The Rebirth of Rapunzel

A Mythic Biography of the Maiden in the Tower

Kate Forsyth

First published in Australia in 2016
by FableCroft Publishing

http://fablecroft.com.au

Cover artwork and design by Kathleen Jennings
Design and layout by Tehani Wessely
Typeset in Sabon MT Pro and IM Fell DW Pica

National Library of Australia Cataloguing-in-Publication entry

Creator: Forsyth, Kate, 1966– author.
Title: The rebirth of Rapunzel : a mythic biography of the maiden in the tower / Kate Forsyth.
ISBN: 9780992553494 (hardback)
9780994469007 (ebook)
Notes: Includes bibliographical references.
Subjects: Rapunzel (Tale)—History and criticism.
Mythology in literature.
Dewey Number: 398.2

Kate would like to thank her supervisors, Debra Adelaide, Sarah Gibson, Tegan Bennett Daylight and Delia Falconer for all their patient help and advice during her doctoral studies, as well as her doctoral markers, Lisa Bennett, Van Ikin and Rosie Dub. She would also like to thank her publishers, Random House Australia, Allison & Busby UK, St Martin's Press USA, and Hemiro Ltd Russia, for all their support in the publication of her novel *Bitter Greens*.

The publisher gratefully acknowledges the generous assistance given to the production of this book by Elizabeth Disney. She would also like to thank Dr Sean Williams and Dr Kim Wilkins for inspiration and remembering, respectively.

ALSO FROM FABLECROFT PUBLISHING…

Cranky Ladies of History edited by Tansy Rayner Roberts and Tehani Wessely

Phantazein edited by Tehani Wessely

To Spin a Darker Stair by Catherynne Valente and Faith Mudge

Contents

SECTION ONE:
The Rebirth of Rapunzel

Introduction

In Search of Rapunzel

'Rapunzel' is one of the best known stories in the classic Western canon of fairy tales. It tells the story of a young woman—named Rapunzel—who is locked away in a tower by a witch. The heroine is named for a plant which her father stole from the witch's walled garden. The only access to Rapunzel is via her own impossibly long hair. A prince climbs the ladder of hair and falls in love with her, setting in motion a chain of events which results in the expulsion of the maiden from her tower, the blinding and subsequent healing of the prince, and the coming together of maiden and prince in the essential 'happy-ever-after' ending.

Most readers of the Western canon of fairy tales are familiar with 'Rapunzel' thanks to its inclusion by the Grimm brothers in their famous collection of fairy tales, first published in 1812 and then edited, emendated, and embellished in later volumes, culminating in the final 1857 imprint. There have been numerous English translations of the Grimm brothers' 1857 version of 'Rapunzel', including one by the writer and translator Lucy Crane in 1882 which was widely republished. It was her version of the tale that I first read as a seven-year-old child, and which began my own personal fascination with Rapunzel.

As a child I used to wonder about the story and imagine myself as the heroine. I first tried to retell it in story form when I was twelve. As an adult, I drew upon its symbols and structures in my creative work, along with the motifs of other favourite fairy tales. It was always 'Rapunzel' that had the most potent meaning for me, however, for reasons which I explore in the first chapter of this exegesis.

I had long wanted to retell 'Rapunzel' in novel form, but found myself held in stasis, unable to move forward with my narrative (rather like Rapunzel herself, trapped in her tower). I began to wonder who had first told the tale. I imagined some wizened old woman (perhaps Rapunzel herself) telling her story to one of the Grimm brothers. However, my search to find the first teller of the tale led me to realise that it is a story which has existed, with many different faces and names, for thousands of years. There are, indeed, so many versions of 'The Maiden in the Tower' tale that it has its own classification in the Aarne-Thompson-Uther fairy tale motif index: Tale Type 310 (Getty 1997). In Chapter 2 of this exegesis, I explore many of these tales, from their possible roots in pre-literate matriarchal mythology through Ancient Greek, Jewish and Persian legends, to the French troubadour tradition, and thence to medieval Christian accounts of imprisoned virgins such as St Barbara.

In the early 1600s, a Neapolitan courtier named Giambattista Basile (1566-1632) included a tale named 'Petrosinella' (meaning 'Little Parsley') in a collection of bawdy stories aimed at amusing the highly educated crowd in which he moved (Canepa 1999). He was arguably familiar with many of the earlier 'Maiden in the Tower' tales and drew upon them to create a new tale of a girl who escapes from her tower with the help of her princely lover and three magical acorns (I discuss his retelling in Chapter 3).

Sixty-three years later, in 1697, a French noblewoman called Charlotte-Rose de Caumont de La Force (1650-1724) created a new collection of fairy tales that included the story 'Persinette' (also meaning 'Little Parsley', and examined in Chapter 4). Although she was clearly influenced by Basile, La Force's version is the first to contain the interlocking chain of causes and consequences, motifs and metaphors, which is widely recognised today as the memeplex of 'Rapunzel'[1]—the theft of forbidden food; the surrender of the child named for the plant; the woman of mysterious magical powers; the maiden locked in the tower; the ladder of golden hair; the seducing prince; the maiden's impregnation; her exile to the wilderness; the blinding of the prince; Rapunzel's healing tears; and the final redemption of the witch.

La Force's tale was retold, first by the German writer Friedrich Schulz in 1790, who re-named it 'Rapunzel', and then by the Grimm brothers in the mid-1800s (explored in Chapter 5). It has continued to be retold right through to contemporary times. In Chapter 6, I appraise key revisionings of the tale by writers such as William Morris, Anne Sexton, Nicholas Stuart Gray, and Donna Jo Napoli, culminating in Disney's 2010 musical fantasy *Tangled*. There are many hundreds of other creative reimaginings of 'Rapunzel' that I wish I had room to explore in this exegesis—paintings, poems, operas, short stories, art installations and advertisements. However, central to this exegesis is my own personal journey towards understanding the 'Rapunzel' fairy tale and its hold on my imagination, and so I have chosen to focus on those reimaginings that most influenced my novel *Bitter Greens*.

In each chapter of this exegesis, I interrogate the many different retellings of 'The Maiden in the Tower' in an attempt to understand why this tale-type has continued to be told and retold over so many centuries. Why has it survived, when so many other stories have been lost and forgotten?

The folklorist Alan Dundes believed that fairy tales, fables and other such narratives spoke in symbolic codes, and that such codes could be deciphered. In order to do so, he recommended the comparison of the motifs of a large number of different versions of a tale type[2], in order to come towards an understanding of their meaning (1980, pp. 187-197).

Guided primarily by Dundes's theories, I have therefore, in this exegesis, brought together for the first time a complete history of the tale, from the mythic fragments that may be proof of its existence in ancient gynocentric oral traditions right through to key contemporary reimaginings. Other scholars have examined these tales in seclusion, or grouped a few of them together, but I believe I am the first to trace the cultural evolution of 'Rapunzel' from ancient tales of three-faced goddesses right through to Disney's *Tangled*.

I was inspired in this task by Stephen Knight's work on Robin Hood and his notion of a 'mythic biography' that 'deals with both the human and the superhuman manifestations and meanings of the figure…who has over centuries and in many places and many genres had a varying but powerful identity' (2003, p. xiii). I have not only used Stephen Knight's term 'mythic biography' in the title of my exegesis but also borrowed his methodology in evaluating the tale through its chronological development, thus creating, in his words, 'a biography of (the myth)' (p. xiii), which is shaped by the socio-historical forces at work in changing human cultures.

In this task, I am particularly indebted to the work of Terri Windling and Laura J. Getty, both of whom have examined the ancestry of Rapunzel in essay form. Other scholars whose work has been of significant help to me include Cristina Bacchilega, Ruth B. Bottigheimer, Jane Caputi, Heide Göttner-Abendroth (and her theories of fairy tales as camouflaged matriarchal myths), Donald Haase, Elizabeth Wanning Harries (her work on the 17th century French female fairy tale tellers was invaluable to me), Heide Heiner (with thanks to her work on 'Rapunzel' type tales around the world), James McGlathery, Maria Tatar, Marina Warner and Jack Zipes, whose work in memetic theory was of particular use for me in helping me understand the reason why such tales continue to be retold and retold (2006, pp. 3-16; 2012, pp. 17-20).

I began my search for Rapunzel for deeper insight into the tale, to inform my own understanding of its meaning and purpose, and to inspire my own creative retelling. However, in the process of researching and writing this exegesis my interest was quickened by the question of why it is 'Rapunzel' which has so haunted my imagination and those of so many other creative artists. Why has this tale of a girl locked away in a tower continued to be told and retold over so many hundreds of years?

My exegesis will argue that this story—like most other fairy tales—carries camouflaged within it ancient mythic structures and symbols. These work at an unconscious level to give the tale a deep psychological resonance. It is my contention that it is the symbolic power of these motifemes that gave the story its lasting appeal, so that the story continues to be of relevance to each new audience. 'Rapunzel' is a story about escape from imprisonment. It tells the transformative journey from stasis and shadows to liberation and light. This makes it a story that reverberates very strongly with any individual—male or female, child or adult—who has found themselves trapped by their circumstances, whether this is caused by the will of another, or their own inability to change and grow.

Fairy tales always work on two levels, Maurice Sendak believed: 'First as stories; secondly, as the unravelling of deep psychological dramas' (in Wintle & Fisher 1974, p. 28). On that deeper psychological level, 'Rapunzel' is a story about a young woman who breaks out of her prison; she rescues herself. This is, I believe, a large part of the secret of the fairy tale's enduring fascination, for myself and for others.

Chapter I

The Golden Braid: Rapunzel and I

I have been haunted by Rapunzel ever since I was a child.

I can remember the very day my obsession began. I was seven years old and my mother gave me a copy of *Grimm's Fairy Tales,* beautifully bound in red leather with romantic old-fashioned drawings by Walter Crane. The book was a gift to comfort me, for I was—once again—to be left alone in hospital.

I began to read the book the moment my mother left me with many kisses and promises that she would see me in the morning. I was sick, in pain, and half-blind. Fever dizzied me. I lay there in the darkness, a small light burning on the page. With one eye covered with a patch, I read my way through the tales in that book. The stories were full of wonder and peril and beauty and strangeness. Some made me smile. Others made me yearn to travel far, far away to lands of shadowy forests and towers hidden behind thorns. One or two made me shiver and huddle deeper into my white hospital blanket. All would come to capture my imagination. I read that book so many times the spine eventually broke, pages falling out like white feathers. Yet of all the tales, it was 'Rapunzel' that enthralled me the most.

The story I read that day was written by Lucy Crane in 1886, from her own translation of the Grimm Brothers' 1857 edition of *Kinder-und-Hausmärchen*. The story began: 'There once lived a man and his wife, who had long wished for a child, but in vain.' Their house overlooked a lush garden overflowing with herbs and flowers and fruit, but no one dared to venture within its high walls for the garden belonged to a witch of great might. Looking into the garden, the woman was overcome by an insatiable desire to eat some of the rampion she saw growing there: 'it looked so fresh and green that she began to wish for some; and at length she longed for it greatly' (Crane 1973, p. 32).

The woman told her husband that she would die if she did not eat some of the witch's rampion, and so he climbed the wall and stole a handful for her. She ate it greedily, and then asked for more. So her husband climbed the wall again, but this time was caught by the witch. With angry eyes, she threatened him then exacted a promise: he must give up his unborn child to her.

In time, a daughter was born and the witch appeared. 'Giving the child the name of Rapunzel (which is the same as rampion), she took it away with her' (p. 34). At the age of twelve, Rapunzel was locked up in a tower in the midst of a wood, with neither steps nor door but only a small window at the top. When the witch wanted to be let into the tower, she called, 'Rapunzel, Rapunzel! Let down your hair' (p. 34), and the girl lowered her impossibly long hair for the witch to climb. One day the King's son rode through the forest and heard Rapunzel singing. Enchanted by her beautiful voice, he followed the sound and discovered the hidden tower. He heard the witch call and watched her clamber up the golden ladder of hair. Once the witch had come down again and gone away, he too called out the words.

Rapunzel let down her hair and the King's son climbed up into the tower. At first she was terrified, but he spoke kindly to her and asked her to take him for her husband. Rapunzel agreed, and told him to bring a silken rope with him each time he came so that she could make a ladder and so escape. The King's son then visited her every evening, until Rapunzel betrayed herself to the witch by unwittingly asking: 'Mother Gothel, how is it that you climb up here so slowly, and the King's son is with me in a moment?' (p. 35).

Enraged, the witch cut off Rapunzel's long braid of hair and cast her out into the wilderness. The witch then lowered the braid to the prince who climbed up the tower, only to be confronted by the furious witch. She mocked him and told him

Rapunzel was lost to him. In an agony of grief, the King's son sprang from the tower. Although he survived the fall, the thorns on which he fell put out his eyes, and he was blinded. 'He wandered several years in misery until at last he came to the desert place where Rapunzel lived with her two twin-children that she had borne, a boy and a girl.' The King's son recognised Rapunzel's voice, and the two were reunited. Rapunzel wept, and her tears fell upon his eyes and healed his blindness. 'Then he took her to his kingdom…and there they lived long and happily' (p. 36).

This fairy tale seemed—to me—full of some kind of potent meaning. As a child, I only dimly grasped why it sang to me. I knew I loved the ardent romance, the vivid images of the tower guarded by thorns and the singing girl with the oriflamme of hair, the miraculous healing of the prince's blinded eyes. But I did not truly understand why it shook and excited me so much. I only knew that 'Rapunzel' was stuck in my imagination like a burr. Perhaps it was because I—like Rapunzel—was trapped in a prison. Hers was a tower with neither door nor stair. Mine was a hospital ward, and I was imprisoned by the pain and loneliness of chronic illness.

The Golden Braid

I was only a child when I faced death for the first time.

Aged just two years and four months, I was savaged by my father's Doberman Pinscher in the back garden of our home in the Artarmon veterinary hospital. As I was tossed like a rag doll, the dog's fangs penetrated straight through the thin bone of my skull and into the brain. My left eye was missed by a fraction of a millimetre. My ear was torn away.

Somehow my mother managed to wrest me from the dog's jaws. She wrapped me in towels and ran for help, my four year old sister Belinda running sobbing beside her. A young man driving down the Pacific Highway stopped and picked her up. At North Shore Hospital, when the nurses unwound the bloody towels from around my head, he fainted.

My mother was told to prepare herself. I was unlikely to live.

Somehow they patched me together again. My ear was sewn back on, albeit a little crookedly. More than two hundred stitches covered my head and face. I must have looked like a tiny Frankenstein's monster.

I did not wake up. My temperature climbed higher and higher, and still I lay unwaking, like a cursed princess. No amount of kisses could rouse me.

Ten days after the accident, red and floppy as a skinned rabbit, I was gripped by relentless fever.

Still no one could wake me. The doctors told my mother I had bacterial meningitis. I think of it as another savage dog, a crazed wolf, pinning me down with its heavy paw. No drugs could release me from its jaws. Prepare yourself, my mother was told. Few children survive meningitis.

I lay in ice like a glass coffin. I was white and red and black. I had gone away from this world, gone somewhere no one could reach me. Days passed and still my fever climbed. My small body convulsed.

It's worse than meningitis, the doctors said. It's meningoencephalitis. A wild whirling word, full of holes and spikes. Other words came. Seizures. Toxic. Fatal. I heard none of them. The doctors wanted to drill a hole through my skull to help drain away the infection sinking its claws into my brain. In 1968, this was a procedure that was nearly always fatal. My mother would not let them. Come back, she said to me. Please come back.

The fever broke. Twenty days after the dog attack, I opened one eye (the other was lost inside a bruised mess of swelling and stitches.) I swallowed some milk. I spoke. A week later I was allowed to go home.

It was not the last time that I would outface death.

The doctors would soon discover that the dog's fang had destroyed my tear duct. My eye wept all the time. I was like a miniature painting of the Mater Dolorosa, or Picasso's Weeping Woman, tears constantly trickling down my face. I developed chronic dacryocystitis (a recurring infection of the tear-duct), resulting in dangerously high fevers, severe swelling, and blindness. As the eye is deeply embedded in the cranium, abscesses of the tear duct are life-threatening once the infection and inflammation begin to affect the delicate tissues of the brain. From the age of three years to the age of eleven, I was constantly in and out of hospital.

I could hear the fever coming, a rattling roaring locomotion rushing upon me. I could feel it in my skin. Whitecaps of flame and frost. My body undulating, shrinking, stretching. Fingers like tentacles. Whirling embers in my eyes. Demonic faces mocking me.

I lay in the narrow hospital bed with a patch over my bad eye, gazing out the window. All I could see was a green hill crested with an immense tree and what looked like a castle. I used to imagine galloping up that green hill on the back of a white horse that would fling out its great wings, leap into the air, and take me away.

Stories were my only consolation. I would read all day and as late into the night as the nurses would let me. I dreaded the light being turned off, I dreaded the empty hours of the night. Once my book was taken away from me, all I could do was lie there in pain, trying to imagine myself back in its pages.

The Rebirth of Rapunzel

By the time my mother gave me 'Rapunzel' to read, I had spent the better part of my childhood in hospital. I felt a great affinity with that other young girl, locked away alone in a tower as I was confined alone in my hospital ward. I loved the way her tears had healed the prince's blindness and wished that my own tears, weeping constantly from my damaged tear duct, would heal mine. I told myself: One day I too shall escape. One day I too shall be healed.

In time, of course, I was. At the age of eleven, I became the first Australian to have a successful implantation of an artificial tear duct. A small glass tube, called a Jones tube, was inserted beside my eye, draining fluids down the back of my throat.

So I escaped my tower, my tears healed.

I had already begun to write my own stories. By the age of ten, I had written two novels, longhand in old exercise books. The first was called 'Runaway'. The second was called 'Far, Far Away'. Unsurprisingly, both deal with themes of escape.

When I was twelve, I read *The Stone Cage*, a 1963 retelling of 'Rapunzel' by the British children's author, Nicholas Stuart Gray, told from the point of the view of the witch's cat. I began to imagine writing my own retelling of Rapunzel before I had even finished reading the book. I loved *The*

Stone Cage, yet I felt the story should have been told from Rapunzel's point of view. It should have given some sense of the terrible loneliness, fear and despair she must have endured.

When I was fourteen, I read *Till We Have Faces: A Myth Retold*, by C.S. Lewis. Dark and strong and full of anger, it showed how well-known tales—in this case, the story of Cupid and Psyche—could be turned utterly inside-out when told from the point of view of the supposed villain of the tale.

As I grew into adulthood, I kept on reading fairy tale retellings and wrote novels in which appear—again and again—themes of imprisonment and escape, blindness and healing, roses and thorns, flight and falling. Towers were a common motif, as was hair as a symbol of life and renewal. Some of my novels were written for adults and some for children, but all of them drew upon fairy tale motifs and themes.

Then, the children's writer Garth Nix gave me an old, hard-back edition of *The Stone Cage* for my fortieth birthday. I read the novel again, and was vividly reminded of my own childhood fascination with 'Rapunzel' and how I had first tried to rewrite the story when I was twelve. I began to wonder about the story again. Why did the witch lock Rapunzel in a tower? Why didn't the prince bring Rapunzel a rope? How did her hair grow so long? Did she ever find her true parents again? What happened to the witch afterwards? I was troubled by the lacunae in the story, the gaps and holes and tatters. I began to cobble these holes together in my mind, weaving a new cloth of fancy.

At last I knew I had to write my own retelling of 'Rapunzel'. Not as a children's book, I thought. 'Rapunzel' is a story about sexual desire and obsession and cruelty. It had to be a novel for adults. I also did not want to write it as an otherworldly fantasy. I wanted to capture the charge of terror and despair that young girl must have felt. I wanted to remind readers that women have been locked up for centuries against their wills in this world.

Our world.

So I decided to set *Bitter Greens,* my Rapunzel retelling, in a real place at a real time. This decision meant I could not use magic to explain all the mysteries in the story—the tower without a door or a stair, the golden fathoms of her hair, the tears that heal the prince's eyes…my imagination caught fire.

But where and when would I set my story? I began to look at the historical roots of the tale, to find earlier versions of the story that might help me. I discovered that one of the earliest versions of 'Rapunzel' was written in the early 1600s by Giambattista Basile, a courtier employed as a soldier by the Venetian Republic. I was at once inspired by the possibilities of setting my 'Rapunzel' retelling in Venice, that city of towers and walled gardens and narrow canals.

Yet Basile's tale had a different ending. His heroine escapes with the prince and throws three magical acorns over her shoulder that transform into savage animals that first impede and then devour the witch. It was the ending with the healing tears that spoke so powerfully to me. I wanted to know who first told that tale. I had to dig deeper.

I kept on reading and researching, and one day stumbled upon an essay by Terri Windling called 'Rapunzel, Rapunzel, Let Down your Hair' (2007). It examined the ancestry of the tale from Basile onwards, and included a brief summary of the life of the next writer to retell the story. She was the 17th century French writer Charlotte-Rose de Caumont de La Force, whose tale 'Persinette' is the first to contain the ending with the motif of the healing tears that was to become crystallised as the tale we know as 'Rapunzel'. La Force's collection of fairy tales *Les Contes des Contes* was published in Paris by Simon Benard on 23 December 1697, six months after Charles Perrault's collection. It included eight other tales including 'L'Enchanteur', 'Tourbillon', and 'La Bonne Femme' (Raynard (ed.) 2012, p. 91).

La Force was an active participant in the Parisian salons where it was the fashion to create a 'fairy tale' to be told to an audience of well-educated and sophisticated noblemen and noblewomen. The term 'conte de fees' was coined by another of these storytellers, Marie-Catherine Le Jumel de Barneville, the Baroness d'Aulnoy, and such tellers of tales were called *conteuses* if they were women and *conteurs* if they were male. Perrault was one such teller, and so was his niece, Marie-Jeanne L'Héritier de Villandon. Another well-known *conteuse* of the day was La Force's cousin Henriette-Julie de Murat.

In France, in the late 17th century, noblewomen such as La Force had very little control over their lives. They were largely forbidden to own property and marriages were arranged on their behalf to strengthen the financial and political position of their families. 'Sex was a husband's legal right,' Windling wrote (2007, p. 1):

> and there was no possibility of divorce. Young girls could find themselves married off to men many years their senior or of vile temper and habits; disobedient daughters could be shut away in convents or locked up in mad-houses. Little wonder, then, that French fairy tales are filled with girls handed over to various wicked creatures by cruel or feckless parents, or locked up in enchanted towers where only true love can save them.

La Force was one of those disobedient women shut away in a convent, though it was her second cousin Louis XIV who decreed her banishment. She had outraged the King with a series of flagrant love affairs and by the publication of erotic novels and blasphemous songs. In one scandalous episode, La Force dressed up as a dancing bear to gain access to her younger lover. It was while she was locked away from the world in the nunnery that La Force wrote her collection of fairy tales, one of the first in the French tradition.

I was at once struck by the symbolic parallels between the fictional story of 'Persinette' and the true life story of its teller: both were imprisoned against their will; both had caused outrage because of a forbidden love affair; and both longed for escape. I at once began to see how I could frame my own reimagining of the 'Rapunzel' fairy tale with a fictionalised account of La Force's life.

I also felt a strong connection to La Force herself. Like me, she was a writer and an oral storyteller with a love of history and fairy tales. She was a proto-feminist who fought against the narrow societal strictures of her time, wanting to live her own life, and write and love as she pleased. Known for her numerous lovers and her bold wit and wicked charm, she scandalised the royal court with her beliefs and behaviour. That rebellious free spirit is woven through all her remarkable tales. From the moment I first read about La Force, I knew I wanted to write about her.

Yet she turned out to be little more than a footnote in fairy tale studies. It took me a long time to find out more than the few paragraphs that were included in Windling's essay. Eventually, I managed to track down a biography of her life, *Mademoiselle de La Force: un auteur méconnu du* XVIIe *siècle*, by the French academic Michel Souloumiac. I enlisted the help of a French translator, Sylvie Poupard-Gould, who not only rendered into English the whole of Souloumiac's work but also translated an autobiographical sketch written by La Force, plus a number of her fairy tales which had never before been adapted into English[3]. I also scoured the letters and diaries of courtiers of the time[4], and searched for her between the lines of non-fiction books written about the court of the Sun King[5]. The more I found about her, the more interesting her story became. La Force was, I thought, one of the most fascinating women ever forgotten by history.

I began to envision a novel in which she was one of my three primary narrative threads, along with the maiden-in-the-tower and the witch. I saw the three narrative strands being woven together like a braid, symbolically representing the impossibly long plait of golden hair, which is the most visually arresting image in the tale.

My novel *Bitter Greens* begins with Charlotte-Rose's story. (To differentiate between the real and the imagined woman, I shall call my fictional character by her first name, Charlotte-Rose, as I do in the novel, and the real woman by her last name, La Force). It is January 1697, and the King has ordered Charlotte-Rose to a nunnery. The poverty-stricken convent of Gercy-en-Brie is far away from Paris and all that she holds dear. Charlotte-Rose is stripped of her luxurious court dress of golden silk, and made to give up all of her material possessions, which include her precious writing tools. Her quills are broken, her ink emptied out, her parchment torn to pieces. Charlotte-Rose's hair is also shorn, which was normal practice for novitiates in French convents during the Counter-Reformation. She finds it most difficult to submit her bold and independent spirit to the strict laws of *clausura*, just as I imagine the historical figure of La Force would. One of the nuns, Sœur Seraphina, is the convent apothecary and looks after the nunnery's garden. She takes Charlotte-Rose into the garden and there tells her the story of a girl whose parents had sold her to a sorceress for a handful of bitter greens.

The narrative then moves to the point of view of Margherita, my maiden-figure, who is the daughter of a mask-maker in Venice in the 1590s. Her mother had asked the help of the sorceress to cast a love spell on her father, and later was smitten by the lush greenness of the plants in the sorceress's garden. The sorceress takes the child at the age of seven to the Ospedale della Pietà, a hospital for abandoned children, where she is taught to sing. At the age of twelve, Margherita is taken by the sorceress and locked in a tower on Lake Garda. Long hanks of red-gold hair are sewn into her own, creating tresses so long they can be used as a rope ladder for the sorceress to climb in and out of the tower. Once she is left alone, Margherita tries to escape and finds entombed in the cellar of the tower the skeletons of eight other girls. She realises that the sorceress has sewn the dead girls' hair into her own.

The narrative then returns briefly to Charlotte-Rose's point of view as she wonders what could possibly drive a woman to lock away a little girl in a tower. Sœur Seraphina tells her the sorceress was afraid of time.

The next section is told from the point of view of the sorceress, who calls herself Selena Leonelli. She is the illegitimate daughter of a Venetian courtesan in the early 1500s. When her mother drinks poison and dies, after being cruelly gang-raped, Selena is left alone. She seeks out a well-known local witch named Sibillia to help her cast a curse on the man who ordered her mother's rape. The witch takes her on as an apprentice, and Selena learns her dark arts and exacts her revenge.

One night, during Carnevale, she meets a young painter named Tiziano who admires her vivid red-gold hair and wishes to paint her (Tiziano is better known by the English rendering of his name, Titian). Then the witch Sibillia dies of the plague and Selena determines that she shall never grow old and die. She becomes a courtesan and Tiziano's mistress and muse, and begins to bathe in the blood of young virgins in order to stay young and beautiful. With the Grand Inquisitor of Venice suspicious of her, Selena finds an old tower on the shores of Lake Garda to keep her red-haired virgins, who—one by one—die, leaving her bereft. In time, her lover Tiziano also dies—at the remarkable age of eighty-eight, unusually old for the times. Selena, however, still looks like she did when he first met her so many years earlier. It is then that Selena meets Margherita's red-haired mother and begins to plot how to trap her into giving up her as-yet-unborn daughter.

The narrative then returns to Charlotte-Rose's point of view. She remembers her own first love affairs at the royal courts of Paris and Versailles and her longing to write. Without money of her own, she must work as a maid-of-honour and cannot afford the time nor the cost of writing. So—in order to try and convince a man to marry her—Charlotte-Rose purchases a love spell from a witch in Paris. This action results in a humiliating scandal that she finds hard to bear. To distract herself from the memory, she asks Sœur Seraphina to continue with her tale of the girl locked in the tower.

Margherita is a child no longer, but a young woman who has adapted to her life in the tower as best she can. One day a young man named Lucio climbs up the ladder of her hair into the tower. They fall in love and into bed. Lucio begs Margherita to run away with him, but she finds that she cannot leave. The sorceress has bound her to the tower.

Eventually she finds a way to break the spell, but as she prepares to escape the sorceress returns. Margherita unwittingly betrays herself and Lucio, revealing that she is with child. The sorceress cuts off Margherita's great length of golden-red hair and raises her knife to strike her.

At that point, the narrative returns to Charlotte-Rose and Sœur Seraphina in the nunnery. The smell of rue on her hands jolts a vivid memory for Charlotte-Rose of the time when she was arrested for her involvement in the bloody Affair of the Poisons, a scandal which rocked Paris in the late 1670s and early 1680s. The Parisian witch La Voisin who had sold Charlotte-Rose the love spell proves to have also been selling poisons and arranging abortions, and anyone who is connected to her—including Charlotte-Rose—ends up in prison. Although La Voisin and many others are burnt to death, Charlotte-Rose is freed. She then falls in love with a much younger man and, when his family locks him away in a castle, dresses up a dancing bear to rescue him. They marry, but his father has the marriage annulled and Charlotte-Rose is charged with interfering with a minor (her husband Charles was twenty-four). He is sent away to fight in the king's wars and she never sees him again.

It may be worth noting here that each of these dramatic events in Charlotte-Rose's life was inspired by true events in La Force's. She was implicated in the Affair of the Poisons, she did disguise herself in a bearskin to see her young lover, and she was put on trial and found guilty of seducing a minor.

In the final section of Margherita's narrative, she outwits the sorceress Selena and traps her in the tower. Margherita then escapes into the wild, desolate mountains where, all alone, she gives birth to twin children. Meanwhile, Lucio has climbed the tower but finds the sorceress there instead of his lover. He falls from the tower height and is blinded. Margherita searches for him and, when she has found him, weeps. Her tears fall on his eyes and wash away the crusted blood so that he can see again. Margherita then forgives the witch and frees her from the tower, and then returns to Venice to find her lost parents. Finally, Margherita and Lucio go to Florence where she sings the role of Proserpina in Jacopo Peri's *Euridice*, the first opera ever staged.

In the final section of the novel, Charlotte-Rose discovers the secret identity of Sœur Seraphina and begins to write 'Persinette', the story which will make her name and enable her to buy her way free from the convent. The final line is: 'It was by telling stories that I would save myself.'

By the time I had finished writing *Bitter Greens*, my fascination with the 'Rapunzel' fairy tale had developed into a full-blown obsession. I had read everything I could find on the subject[6]. I discovered that—although the story as it is best known was written with quill and ink by a 17th century noblewoman—the taproot of the tale ran far back into the mythic past, into primeval stories of death and rebirth, sacrifice and redemption, of which only fragments remain in Neolithic art and sculpture.

I found that taproot had sprouted many other story saplings, found in ancient Western myths and legends, and in Christian, Jewish and Islamic narrative traditions. I collected and read these tales, and compared their motifs and thematic structures, and wondered about their evolution through oral storytelling traditions to the recorded literary tales of Basile, La Force, and the Grimms. I also hunted down and read many hundreds of 'Rapunzel' retellings.

I became particularly interested in the possible meaning of the tale's motifs, those images and incidents which make the story so memorable and yet so mysterious. Like all retellers of a tale, I had to decide how to interpret and employ these motifs. I also began to wonder why it was that the 'Rapunzel' fairy tale held such power for me, and for the other many retellers of the tale. In thinking about these questions, I grew interested in mimetic theory as a way of recognising and understanding the cultural transmission of fairy tales, thanks to my reading of fairy tale scholar Jack Zipes' work on this matter.

To explain 'Why Fairy Tales Stick' (2006), Zipes drew upon the work of evolutionary biologist Richard Dawkins in his 1976 book, *The Selfish Gene,* which compares a 'meme' (an infectious unit of cultural information such as a nursery rhyme, a recipe, or a way of building an arch which is transmitted by repetition and replication) to the biological transmission of genes. According to Zipes, a fairy tale can be described as a 'memeplex'—an interconnected string of scenes and symbols that together assist in the survival of the story. It is passed from mind to mind, over generations and/or over geographies, as infectiously as any virus. Along the way, the story helps to shape sociogenic mindsets and attitudes, and allows the memorisation of culturally engraved lessons (Zipes 2006, pp. 2-13).

It is widely accepted that stories have been told as long as humans have had spoken language, and that such tales performed an important pedagogical function in the culture in which they were told. Marina Warner has written: 'fairy tales exchange knowledge between an older voice of experience and a younger audience, they present pictures of perils and possibilities that lie ahead, they use terror to set limits on choice and offer consolation to the wronged, they draw social outlines around boys and girls, fathers and mothers, the rich and the poor, the rulers and the ruled...they stand up to adversity with dreams of vengeance, power and vindication' (1994, p. 21).

As the influential folklorist Alan Dundes has written: 'Folklore *means* something—to the tale teller, to the song singer, to the riddler, and to the audience...Folktales...have passed the test of time, and are transmitted again and again. Unlike individual dreams, folktales must appeal to the psyches of many, many individuals if they are to survive' (1980, pp. 33-34).

Zipes believes a meme must be relevant if it is to be passed on (2012, p. 19), while the English psychologist Susan Blackmore has said that memes are only successful if they are emotionally charged and easily memorable (1999, pp. 55-57). Similarly, Walter Burkert, a German professor of mythology and religious cults, has written: 'a tale becomes traditional not by virtue of being created, but by being retold and accepted...' (quoted in Zipes 2012, p. 7). Burkert then elaborates: 'A tale "created"—that is, invented by an individual author—may somehow become "myth" if it becomes traditional...(but only if the tale) has the pragmatic function of solving a problem' (quoted in Zipes 2012, p. 38).

In other words, a story such as 'Rapunzel' only survives if it is retold, and it is only retold if it is both memorable and relevant, articulating some desire or dilemma in both the teller and the audience.

The tale's motifs—the walled garden with its tempting green vegetation, the dark sorceress who traps a yearning mother into unnatural longings, the girl with the impossibly long golden hair, the soaring tower guarded by thorns, the blinded prince groping his way through the wilderness—these are all most memorable. Yet what desire do these scenes and characters articulate? What dilemmas do they illuminate?

In order to explore these questions, I have drawn upon Dundes's structural approach to analysing folktales which calls for the comparison of tale variants and the analysis of individual motifemes for their mythical foundations. In his theory, a motifeme is a unit of a narrative plot which manifests itself as a motif. For example, a common motifeme would be Interdiction + Violation + Consequence (Green 1997, p. 565). In 'Rapunzel', this manifests itself as Walled Garden + Theft of Plant + Surrendering of Child. I have therefore looked closely at the key motifs in the tale in order to understand why they continue to be relevant in contemporary Western society.

To compare the many tale variants, I have, in the following chapters, constructed a 'mythic biography', to use Robin Hood scholar Stephen Knight's term: 'a profile of both the mythological figure and the myth itself' (2003, p. xiii) which aims to not only 'chart the topography of the (tale) but also tried to plumb its meaningful depths, to explore the myth itself' (p. xvi). Knight set out to examine not only the history of Robin Hood, and its chronological evolution through a multiplicity of variants, but also to interrogate the vitality and endurance of the legend to the various cultures in which it was told and re-told, and the figure's mythic resonance within those cultures.

Rapunzel similarly continues to live in contemporary popular culture, as vital as she ever was. And so, in constructing this 'mythic biography' of the maiden in the tower and the many ways she has continued to be retold and reborn, I aim to illuminate—for the first time—the chronology of the tale, its relevance to each new reteller, and the metaphorical and numinous meanings of the tale's motifs which ensure the tale's survival.

As one of those retellers, the act of creating this mythic biography has also allowed me to understand more clearly my own many intuitive and unconscious choices in writing *Bitter Greens*. I wrote my Rapunzel retelling not fully aware of what I was trying to do, yet constantly aware of what I saw as the inner truth of the tale, heard only with the inner ear. Jane Yolen has written: 'Without meaning, without metaphor, without reaching out to touch human emotion, a story is a poor thing: a few rags upon a stick masquerading as a living creature' (2000, p. 24). My aim in writing *Bitter Greens* was to make Rapunzel a living thing, and that is now also my purpose in writing this exegesis.

As Knight wrote: 'the hero of a mythic biography is not dead' (p. xv).

Chapter 2

Maidens in Towers: The Ancestors of Rapunzel

Trying to discover the origin of any fairy tale is a little like trying to find out who invented meatballs, as Angela Carter once famously wrote (1990, pp. ix-x). Like myths, fairy tales are shape-shifters.

Many scholars of fairy tales—from Aarne to Zipes—agree that they have their roots deeply buried in oral and mythic traditions, quite possibly reaching back to the very formation of human speech (Jones 2002, p. xii). These stories were told and retold by parents to their children, who then told them to their own children in turn. They were told by older men and women to the younger generation as they worked at the spinning wheel and the loom, or in the fields and forge, to help hasten the long hours of labour. They were told by travelling storytellers to crowds gathered around a fire in a lord's great hall, or in the village square on market day. They were told by nurses and nannies to their aristocratic charges at bedtime, and acted out on stage by actors in garish costumes and masks (Darnton 1985, pp. 16-17; Jones 2002, pp.

1-6; Warner 1994, pp. xxi-xxiv; Zipes 2006, pp. 52-57). Each time a story was told, it would change just a little. Details would be added for humorous or dramatic effect, or forgotten and lost. Sometimes two or more stories would be woven together, the most vivid images and motifs the ones that would be remembered. As J.R.R. Tolkien has said, 'The Cauldron of Story has always been boiling, and to it have continually been added new bits, dainty and undainty' (1997, p. 125).

It is therefore difficult to know what form the earliest 'Maiden in the Tower' tales may have taken. Mircea Eliade, an authority on the symbolic language of the world's religions, has written that folk and fairy tales, though long a literature of diversion and escape, still contain within them mythological structures and symbols. Examples include initiatory ordeals such as battles with monsters, impossible tasks, riddles to be solved, descent into Underworld-like landscapes, and, finally, marriage with the princess. Mythic characters and motifs therefore remain within folk and fairy tales, camouflaged but enduringly powerful. He uses a striking metaphor to express this idea. Fairy tales, he wrote, are 'an easy doublet' for myths (quoted in Zipes 1994, p. 2), meaning that they are a brightly coloured garment that slips easily over the older garment.

Zipes has interpreted his comments to mean that individual imaginations may have deliberately camouflaged the structures and symbols of myth into secular folk tales for their own purposes, transforming 'the supernatural into magical and mysterious forces that could change their lives' (p. 3). One purpose may have been to preserve old beliefs and wisdoms as new religions imposed their own thought systems upon a conquered society.

The German feminist scholar Heide Göttner-Abendroth also believes that fairy tales are 'veiled myth' (1995, p. 136). She sees the remnants of a lost matriarchal mythology hidden within many Western narrative traditions. In Göttner-Abendroth's book *The Goddess and her Heros* (1995), she puts forward the theory that there were once matriarchal societies in the Indo-European region that believed in a Great Goddess who manifested herself in three faces. The first was the Maiden, the goddess of spring and new growth. Her realm was the heavens, the high places. The second was the Woman, the goddess of summer and fertility. Her realm was the earth and all living things upon it. The third was the Crone, a wintry goddess of death. Her realm is the Underworld, where all living things must travel and be transformed before they can return once more to the light (p. xxi-xxii).

Another key figure in these ancient, lost, matriarchal myths, according to Göttner-Abendroth, is the *heros*, the mortal consort of the Goddess. The hero must suffer through some kind of initiation rite to be worthy of becoming the Sacred King and the lover of the Maiden Goddess. As spring turns into summer and the Maiden becomes Woman, the Sacred King is her consort and the land becomes fertile. At the onset of winter, however, he is sacrificed, sometimes literally and sometimes symbolically, by the Crone Goddess and must journey to the Underworld. The following spring, he is reborn or reawakened, usually with the help of the Maiden. In these ancient belief systems, time was therefore seen as circular, rather than linear: the seasonal cycle of growth, death and rebirth repeating itself endlessly (p. xxii). Göttner-Abendroth believes this narrative sequence of initiation, marriage, death and rebirth was first told in pre-literate Indo-European Palaeolithic and Neolithic cultures—around 7,000 years ago—the evidence captured only in a language of ritual stone carvings and paintings (p. xvi).

The ancient sacred narratives were transformed and camouflaged, Göttner-Abendroth believes, under the patriarchal forces of Christianity. 'Eroticism...was condemned in favour of the principle of universal chastity, and the female figures were accordingly reinterpreted: sin and seduction emanate from every woman who refuses to relinquish her eroticism' (p. 237).

Consequently, the Mother Goddess became simply the mother, then a step-mother or a witch. Her Maiden aspect became a princess, or a much-hated step-daughter. The Sacred King became a prince, or even a tinker or a tailor. The epic cycle of initiation, sacred marriage, descent into the Underworld and return, became simplified and de-mythologised.

Göttner-Abendroth is not the first to postulate such theories, with the poet and scholar Robert Graves famously speculating on the possibility of such ancient matriarchal myths in his much celebrated and much criticised work, *The White Goddess*, first published in 1948. He in turn was drawing upon the work of Jane Harrison, James Frazer and Margaret Murray. More recently, the archaeologist Marija Gimbutas has written extensively in *The Civilization of the Goddess* (1993) on the many images of goddess-like figures found in Palaeolithic and Neolithic burial sites which, she argues, depicted a single universal Great Goddess. It must be noted, however, that her work has been widely criticised, though none of it has been disproved (Talalay 1999).

Göttner-Abendroth examined a number of well-known fairy tales such as 'Mother Holle', 'Hansel and Gretel', 'Cinderella', 'Sleeping Beauty', and 'Snow White', and concluded 'the unwavering precision of the fairy tale sequences demonstrates nothing more than our matriarchal goddess-*heros*-structure' (1995, p. 136). In her examination of 'Cinderella', for example, Göttner-Abendroth wrote: 'The episodes that reflect Cinderella's relationship to her (dead) mother...are filled with beauty and magic and make the whole story possible' (p. 142). Cinderella has planted a hazel twig on her mother's grave which grows into a magical tree filled with talking doves—'Aphrodite's birds'—which assist her in the impossible tasks imposed on her by her dark and terrifying step-mother (a crone-like figure). 'Planting the magic sapling...is a relic of matriarchal arts which (Cinderella) must learn because...(her) real task is not to clean house.' Gifts of a golden dress and golden slippers (the colour of the sun) fall from the hazel tree which grows from the grave, realm of the Underworld. 'In the end, Cinderella is the triumphant, rejuvenated image of the Goddess herself' (p. 143).

Göttner-Abendroth's theories of suppressed matriarchal myths concealed within the structure of fairy tales have had a wide impact on contemporary feminist re-readings of many tales (Haase 2004, p. 15). Zipes wrote in *Fairy Tales and the Art of Subversion*: 'Heide Göttner-Abendroth has demonstrated convincingly... that the matriarchal worldview and motifs of... original folktales underwent successive stages of "patriarchlization"' (2012, p. 7).

In the instance of the 'Cinderella' story, for example, Zipes has argued that residues of the matriarchal tradition are found in each of the first three major incarnations of the tale by

Giambattista Basile, Charles Perrault and the Grimm brothers (quoted in Haase 2004, p. 15-16). Similarly, Louise Bernikow has argued that 'Cinderella' celebrates 'the powerful connection between mother and daughter, who are pitted against a woman compromised by patriarchy' (quoted in Haase 2004, p. 16), while Huang Mei asserts that Cinderella 'does express her will and take the initiative at the crucial events of her life' (quoted in Haase 2004, p. 34). These views are in stark contrast to earlier feminist readings of the tale which saw Cinderella as a 'victim-soul...passive, waiting patiently to be rescued' (Kolbenschlag 1979, p. 75).

Intrigued by Göttner-Abendroth's writings, I came to wonder if 'Rapunzel' could also be analysed to show evidence of such suppressed or camouflaged matriarchal myths. I chose to examine La Force's 1697 tale 'Persinette', which—as discussed earlier—is the first to link together the complete chain of scenes and symbols which is today widely recognised as the memeplex of 'Rapunzel'.

The heroine of the tale begins as a maiden, kept virginal in a high place. Symbolically, she is closely linked to ideas of gardens and new growth and plants, having been exchanged for a handful of green leaves, and having been named for those green leaves. Even her golden hair, growing with such fecundity, can be seen as a symbol of life and strength and regeneration. The maiden is kept in stasis by the crone, the chthonic goddess of death and darkness. She cannot yet move forward in the cycle of life and seasons. She needs the coming of the hero to begin the ritual of love, death, and renewal.

The hero undergoes an initiatory rite in his quest to woo her, forcing his way through the tangled forest and then climbing the rope of impossibly long golden hair up the tower's height. The two consummate their Sacred Marriage and the maiden becomes a woman, impregnated with twins. The heroine is symbolically wounded by the crone, her hair (a symbol of life and the thread of fate) being cut by shears. The hero is literally wounded by the crone, falling from the tower and having his eyes put out by thorns. Blindly he wanders in the wilderness, in eternal darkness, a symbolic death and journey to the Underworld. The heroine undertakes her own similar journey, having been exiled to the wilderness where she gives birth to her children, a son and a daughter. It is only after a period of suffering and despair that the hero and heroine find each other. The hero's reawakening to life and light occurs because of the healing tears of maiden-become-mother, and the two become consorts, ruling together. The crone, meanwhile, is herself redeemed by the story's end, having undergone her own journey through darkness to light.

Laid out in this sequential order, it is indeed possible to see, in 'Persinette', the crucial personages and narrative patterns of Great Goddess myths as conjectured by Göttner-Abendroth. It is fascinating to wonder if the well-known story of 'Rapunzel' is indeed 'veiled myth', and so many thousands of years old.

When I began work on my novel *Bitter Greens*, I had never heard of Göttner-Abendroth, though I was very familiar with the concept of the Triple-Faced Goddess, and had read James Frazer's *The Golden Bough*, Robert Graves' *The White Goddess*, and many other books that deal with the idea of threefold goddesses and muses.

The early drafts of *Bitter Greens* featured an old woman telling her story to the Grimm Brothers. I thought she might be Rapunzel herself. I knew that the 'Rapunzel' sections of the book would be set in and around Venice in the 1600s. At that point, I knew of Basile's story 'Petrosinella', but had not yet discovered La Force and her tale 'Persinette'. I was still fumbling my way forward in darkness, unsure of how to build my narrative.

It is difficult to write a novel full of action, drama, spectacle and suspense when one's heroine is a prisoner. As a result, I began to write *Bitter Greens* from the point of view of the witch, with the following chapters from the point of view of the prince. I wrote more than 30,000 words but became increasingly dissatisfied with the direction my story was taking. Eventually I stopped. For quite some length of time, I was unable to move forward. I was, like Rapunzel herself, held in stasis.

After a series of sleepless nights and troubled days, I realised what was holding me back. 'Rapunzel' is largely a story about feminine power. The key narrative arc is about a girl-child being dominated by her mother-figure, growing up and breaking free, but then finding herself a mother too, in time. It's the women who count in 'Rapunzel': the mother who gives up her daughter for a handful of bitter greens, the witch who locks her in the tower, the girl who gives birth to her twins in the wilderness by herself. Three women, three stories.

I threw out every word I had written and began again. I realised that I needed three narrative strands, and that only the women of the tale would be given a voice. I decided that I would give two of those voices to the maiden and the witch. It would have been a simple and rather obvious choice to give the third voice to Rapunzel's mother. She too had a key role to play in the psychological drama of the tale. However, I chose instead to give that voice to the teller of the tale, even though I did not yet know who this was. This last narrative position was important to me, I think, because

I too am a storyteller. I was trying, intuitively, to express something about my passionately held beliefs about the importance of story. I, like the Shakespearean scholar Harold Goddard, believe that the destiny of the world is determined less by the battles that are lost and won than by the stories it loves and believes in (2009, p. 208).

At this point in my creative journey, I had begun to see in my mind's eye the stories of my witch (a Venetian courtesan) and my maiden (the poor daughter of a Venetian mask-maker and his foundling wife). However, the third narrative point of view in my story was still murky to me. I felt I had to know more about the sources of the story. During the day, I worked on writing the scenes I knew, and at night I began to investigate Rapunzel's ancestry. My research sparked many ideas which worked their way into my writing, both thematically and symbolically, giving me a fresh insight into the importance of the story's key motifs. It also helped confirm for me the importance of choosing a structure for my novel which would resist the patriarchal weakening of the tale, and reconnect it to its mythological sources.

It took me a long time to discover the many variants of the Maiden in the Tower tale, and to ascertain the tale's slow evolution. In the following pages, I have laid out the most important versions of the tale in chronological order, with a brief analysis of its place in the socio-cultural milieu of the time and an examination of any motifs or elements which link it to the story we now know as 'Rapunzel'. I will then endeavour to show how my new understanding of the tale's origins enriched my own creative responses to the tale.

I began by consulting the Aarne-Thompson-Uther 'Tale Type Motif Index', which is a bibliographic tool designed to help in cases just like mine (Jones 2002, pp. 6-7). The ATU index distils world folk tales and fables down to their simplest narrative units, making it easier for scholars to examine their key motifs, themes, and incidents. The most striking and memorable symbolic image in 'Rapunzel' is that of the maiden locked in the tower, and so that is how she is classified, in 'Tale Type 310: The Maiden in the Tower'.

The folklorist Alan Dundes has identified a number of limitations with the ATU Tale Type Index, in particular its Euro-centrism, its over-simplification of story structures, and the 'overlapping' of meaning between motif and tale type (1997, pp. 195-202). Similarly, the feminist scholar Torbeg Lundell has pointed out the male bias of the ATU, with women being presented as little more than passive beauties (Haase 2007, p. 618). Nonetheless, its very simplicity was of use to me in locating and analysing variants of the

'Maiden in the Tower' tales and assisting me in building a timeline of the evolution of the story.

It seems the first recorded 'Maiden in the Tower' tale appeared in ancient Greek mythology, in the story of 'Danaë and the Golden Shower'. As recounted in the 5th century BC by numerous Greek dramatists including Aeschylus, Sophocles and Euripides, Danaë is locked in a brazen tower by her father, King Acrisius of Argos, following a Delphic prophecy that he would be killed by his daughter's son. However, Zeus visits her in a golden shower of rain and she falls pregnant. Her son, Perseus, grows up to accidentally kill his grandfather (Roman 2010, pp. 128-130). 'Danaë and the Golden Shower' contains only two of the key motifs I have identified in the memeplex of 'Rapunzel'—the maiden and the tower. The most striking difference is that the father locks the maiden away from the world, thus upholding models of patriarchal control and domination. Danaë is often depicted in art with long golden-red hair, however, and the narrative arc follows her transformation from imprisoned virgin to a free and active mother. I am also tempted to see a tenuous symbolic link between the 'golden rain' of Zeus's sperm and Rapunzel's healing tears.

Many centuries later, a similar story appears in Jewish narrative traditions. In 'The Princess in the Tower', first recorded in the 8th century, King Solomon locks his daughter in a tower to thwart a prophecy that says she would marry a poor man within the year. 'He ordered the tower to be built without entrances or doors of any kind...with only a single window in his daughter's chamber, from which she could look out on the sea' (Schwartz 1985, p. 49). A giant eagle brings a poor young poet to the tower, and the princess and the poet fall in love. In time, the princess gives birth to a baby boy. King Solomon 'understood for the first time how vain it was to try to prevent the decrees of Providence from taking place' (p. 51). Again this story involves a daughter's power struggle with her father, and again the girl is locked away in a tower to keep her from giving birth to a child that might challenge her father's patriarchal dominance. The most striking image is that of the tower without 'entrances or doors of any kind,' which seems to prefigure the tower in 'Rapunzel'.

The Islamic story tradition is rich in tales of women confined within the high walls of a harem, due to the cultural practice of providing an enclosed space reserved principally for the women and children of the household. The story of the lovers Rudâbeh and Zal is of particular interest in a study of old tales which critics believe may have influenced the formation of 'Rapunzel' (Daniel & Mahdi 2006, p. 14; Noy, Ben-Amos & Rankel 2006, p. 376; Getty 1997, p. 37; and others). The romance of Rudâbeh and Zal was recounted by the celebrated Persian poet Ferdowsi in his epic poem

'Shâhnâma', written at the end of the 10th century. Also known as 'The Book of Kings', 'Shâhnâma' was composed in order to be performed by professional storytellers in coffee houses and marketplaces all over the Middle East (Foley 2005, p. 267). The princess Rudâbeh was described by Ferdowsi in the following terms: 'About her silvern shoulders two musky black tresses curl, encircling them with their ends as though they were links in a chain' (Ferdowsi 2012, p. iii). The young hero Zal—an albino who had been abandoned on a mountain as a baby—hears of the princess's beauty and travels to her palace, where she is kept closely guarded within her father's harem. While her guards are sleeping, Rudâbeh lets down her tresses to Zal like a long rope. He climbs up her hair and so, scandalously, gains ingress to the forbidden harem[7]. Despite his flouting of the rules of the harem, Zal is permitted to marry Rudâbeh and their son Rostam grows up to become a great Persian hero.

The story of Rudâbeh and Zal seems to be the first time in recorded narrative history that a woman's hair was used—or offered—as a means of gaining access to her. As we all know, the hair ladder is a key motif in 'Rapunzel' tales, and so this story from an epic 10th century Persian poem is an important step in the building of the 'Rapunzel' memeplex. It is also fascinating to see one face of Rapunzel—usually depicted so white-skinned and golden-haired—as a dusky-haired, olive-skinned woman from the Middle East.

Medieval romances were rich with tales of damsels in distress and princesses in towers. Perhaps the most famous is the late 12th century story of Floris and Blanchefleur, both born on the same day during a festival of flowers (Hibbard 1963, p. 184). Floris is the son of the Moorish king of Andalusia and Blanchefleur is the daughter of a Christian widow. Afraid his son is falling in love with the beautiful Christian girl, the king sells her to an emir and she is confined within his Tower of Maidens. Floris sets out to rescue Blanchefleur, and gains access to the tower by playing chess with the watchman and returning all his winnings to him until the watchman is forced to give him a favour. Floris is smuggled into the tower in a basket of flowers, and—after a few mishaps—is reunited with Blanchefleur. They are discovered in bed together, but the emir is so moved by the courage and fidelity of the young lovers that they are forgiven and allowed to marry (p. 184).

In this medieval romance, the motifs of maiden, tower and prince appear together with the symbology of vegetation for the first time—Blanchefleur means 'white flower' and Floris means 'flourishing' or 'blossoming', and the hero hid in a basket of flowers. It is also the first time we see the hierarchal class system reversed, with the hero being of noble birth and the heroine coming from a much lower socio-economic stratum. In the earlier 'Maiden in the Tower' tales, the heroine had been a princess and the hero had been a poor poet or a foundling (the exception to this is, of course, 'Danaë and the Golden Shower' in which the seducer was Zeus himself).

In Christian narratives, the motif of a maiden locked in a tower is most strongly associated with the legendary Saint Barbara of Nicomedia (Lanzi & Lanzi 2004, p. 95). Barbara's father, a heathen named Dioscorus, locks her in a tower to remove her from the reach of suitors. She secretly converts to Christianity and, when her father travels away on a journey, orders three windows to be inserted into her bathhouse instead of two, to honour the Holy Trinity. When her father discovers her faith, he declares she shall be put to death. Barbara escapes by passing through the walls of the tower, but is hunted down by her father. Tortured for her Christian beliefs, her wounds miraculously heal overnight and her dark cell is bathed in light. Her own father wishes to be the one to execute her, but when he seizes hold of her long golden hair to hack off her head with his sword, her locks burst into flames. He manages to behead her, nonetheless, but is then struck and killed by lightning (p. 95).

Most images of Saint Barbara show her with a tower in the background and long flowing golden hair, foreshadowing generations of illustrations of Rapunzel that have adorned the covers of countless retellings of the tale. However, Saint Barbara differs from other 'Maiden in the Tower' tales by the lack of the loss of her virginity. There is neither poet nor prince to seduce her, apart from her symbolic marriage to the ideals of Christianity.

Nonetheless, the story of Saint Barbara can be seen to be influential in the evolution of 'Rapunzel' because of the wide popularity of this story in Western Europe from the 14th century onwards. This rise in fame may have been encouraged by her inclusion by the Venetian-born writer Christine de Pizan in *The Book of the City of Ladies,* published around 1405 (Snodgrass 2006, p. 109).

De Pizan was born in Venice in 1364, but lived in Paris after her father won a position at the court of the French king, Charles V. In her mid-thirties, her husband died from bubonic plague and de Pizan provided for her young son and daughter by writing poems, songs, stories and philosophic narratives. She was, it has been conjectured, the first woman to earn her living by her pen (Brown-Grant 1999), and must have been an inspiration to later women writers such as La Force.

Mary Ellen Snodgrass, the author of the *Encyclopedia of Feminist Literature,* has identified de Pizan's story of Saint Barbara as a 'prototype' for the 'Rapunzel' fairy tale (2006, p. 109). *The Book of the City of Ladies* may have had greater impact on later writers of the tale than those earlier mythic variants, due to its immense popularity. It was read by queens, princesses, and noblewoman as well as scholars, and was disseminated widely throughout Europe (Willard 1984). Her work was known to have been read by such luminaries as Marguerite of Austria, Queen Eleanor of Portugal, Mary of Hungary, Louise of Savoy, and Anne of Brittany, twice queen of France (Wilson 1984, p. 339).

By examining these ancestors of Rapunzel in chronological order, it is possible to see how an ancient matriarchal myth may have been recast first as a patriarchal myth, then slowly drained of sacred meaning, its mythic symbols and structures camouflaged by the 'easy doublet' of the medieval romance. The narrative dynamic of the triple-faced goddess became instead a story about a king, a god and a helpless princess. Then—after the passing of many hundreds of years—the god too was drained of power, becoming a poet or a foundling or a prince. The epic cycle of initiation, sacred marriage, descent into the Underworld and return, was simplified and de-mythologised.

Yet, it seems possible to argue that these early 'Maiden in the Tower' tales still managed to retain at their core themes of love, nature, magic, and the erotic which Reneé Lorraine identified as central to a gynocentric aesthetic (1993). The narrative engine of these stories was sensuality and fecundity, their most striking images oncs of golden rain, giant eagles, flowing tresses of hair, baskets of flowers, and lovers entwined together in nakedness. Fear of death and loneliness were cast out by the ecstasy of life-affirming sex and, in most cases, the birth of a child.

It was only in the late Middle Ages that the 'Maiden in the Tower' tale lost even this last remnant of matriarchal mythology. The maiden was not seduced, she did not bear a child, and she did not escape her tower. Instead she was martyred. Murdered by her own father's hand. The images are all patriarchal: lightning, fire, swords. The aftermath is death, desolation and ashes.

Yet, as Chinua Achebe has written, 'The story is everlasting. Like fire, when it is not blazing, it is smouldering under its ashes' (quoted in Yashinsky 2010, p. 6). Glowering under the cinders of these patriarchal myths were the embers of the hag-ridden tales of the ancient past, stories which—as feminist author Jane Caputi has described so eloquently—celebrated 'the monstrous, the female, the feminine, the body, the beast, the erotic, the dark, the green, the earth, and the undercurrents…' (2004, p. 20).

Intuitively I had always recognised that the 'Rapunzel' fairy tale was a story of love and desire and sexual awakening, and that the maiden was symbolically linked to the garden and the plant for which she is named. I had also instinctively recognised the importance of telling part of the tale from the witch's point of view. However, my research into the tale's history brought me a much deeper and richer understanding of the importance of these earthy, erotic associations. I began to deliberately look for ways in which to connect my retelling of the fairy tale to the gynocentric aesthetic of the ancient stories I had discovered.

One way was to foreground forests and gardens and flowers in the story. The walled garden of Charlotte-Rose's mother at their château in Gascony is reflected in the walled garden of the convent in which Charlotte-Rose is incarcerated and the walled garden of the sorceress La Bella Strega in Venice. Images of roses, bees, and healing herbs are repeated throughout the text (I explore this aspect of the tale more deeply in the following chapter).

Most significantly, I began to draw upon the most ancient and hidden aspects of the tale to develop the dramatic arcs of my major characters' journeys of transformation.

At the simplest level, the three heroines of *Bitter Greens* allowed me to represent the three phases of womanhood—Maiden, Woman, Crone—and thus the three-faced aspect of the Great Goddess. However, the story of each of my three characters begins when they are children and follows their lives as they mature into women, and so each embodies their own individual growth towards maturity and wisdom.

The Rebirth of Rapunzel

The story of Charlotte-Rose begins in the spring before her tenth birthday. The king, Louis XIV, came to stay at her home, the Château de Cazeneuve. Charlotte-Rose's boldness displeases him, and as a result her mother, the Baroness de Cazeneuve, is forcibly taken from her home and locked away in a convent. The loss of her mother has a profound effect on Charlotte-Rose and she never forgives the king. At the age of sixteen she is employed as maid of honour to the queen and chafes against the strictures of the gilded cage that is the royal court. Eventually, following a string of scandalous love affairs and escapades (including the delightful episode where she dressed up as a dancing bear in an attempt to free her younger lover), Charlotte-Rose too is incarcerated in a convent, where she must find within herself the strength and courage to change her life.

Margherita's story begins when she is seven and first meets the courtesan known as La Strega Bella (the beautiful witch). She is forcibly taken from her parents and kept locked away in L'Ospedale della Pietà, a Venetian foundling home, till the age of twelve, when she is taken to the tower that shall be her prison for the next five years. She cannot escape this tower until she learns to overcome the bonds of fear that tie her back as strongly as the spell the witch has cast upon her.

The story of the witch, Selena Leonelli, starts when she is eleven and her mother kills herself after being cruelly raped. It follows her apprenticeship to the witch Sibillia, said to be a thousand years old and in hiding from the Inquisition. Selena is bound to the city of Venice by Sibillia and may not leave. As she grows into womanhood and becomes a courtesan like her mother had been, Selena also finds herself imprisoned by her irrational fear of time and death, and, by the end of her tale, she too finds herself locked in the tower.

All three women pass from being virginal girls into sexually active women, and Margherita conceives and gives birth to twins, one of which has fiery-red hair like the sun, the other with hair as dark as night. All three women, in time, find the strength and courage to escape their prisons. Margherita learns to use the witch's own magic against her but, in the end, forgives and releases her. In her final scene, she sings the role of Proserpine, the goddess of spring, in the first ever opera staged in Florence. Selena seeks to make reparation for her evil acts by a life spent as an apothecary, using the natural power of the earth for healing. Charlotte-Rose writes the story she has been told in order to win her own liberation and salvation. All three play out the mythic cycle of initiation, descent into the Underworld, and, ultimately, rebirth and return to the world, and so thus all three are symbolic representations of all three faces of the Great Goddess.

The Rebirth of Rapunzel

My research into the history of the tale helped me realise that I wanted to reclaim the mythic power I had sensed, even as a child, in 'Rapunzel'; to illuminate not only the story itself but what may have been its lost purpose, to teach understanding of the world and the self, and to assist in the difficult transformative journey towards wisdom.

Chapter 3

Walled Gardens: Giambattista Basile & Petrosinella

Giambattista Basile's story 'Petrosinella', published in 1634, was the first tale to bring together many of the key motifs we recognise from 'Rapunzel'—the theft of forbidden food from the walled garden, the witch (in this case, an ogress), the surrendered child, the tower, the ladder of golden hair, the prince, and the seduced maiden. However, the ending was distinctly different from the tale we know: the maiden and the prince escape together, and the girl uses her captor's own magic to defeat and destroy her.

As this chapter will outline, Basile was steeped in the oral storytelling traditions of southern Italy and also likely to have heard, in his travels to Venice and elsewhere, the Jewish and Persian versions of the Maiden in the Tower tale. His story—with its clear traces of older matriarchal myths—was to have a profound influence upon both Charlotte-Rose de la Force's writing and also upon my own, as I will show.

Basile wrote 'Petrosinella' in the early 1600s, while a soldier-of-fortune in service to the Venetian

Republic. He was by nature a man of letters and in his later life would be a courtier in Naples, writing songs, poems and plays for his patrons. 'Petrosinella' was one of a collection of humorous tales called *Lo Cunti de li Cunti* (The Tale of Tales), published in Naples in 1636, four years after his death (Canepa, in Raynard 2012, pp. 25-27).

He was born in 1566 in the small village of Posillipo, not far from Naples which was then one of the largest and most culturally active cities in Europe (Canepa 1999, p. 26). He was born into a poor middle-class family, with a great many brothers and sisters including the composer Lelio Basile, and the celebrated singers Adriana, Margherita and Vittoria Basile. It is believed Basile left Naples in 1599 or early 1600, probably due to his failure to find a patron to fund his literary career. He made his way slowly towards Venice, where he enlisted as a soldier of fortune (Canepa, in Raynard 2012, p. 26).

At the turn of the 17th century, the Most Serene Republic of Venice was a small but powerful city built on small islands in the marshy Venetian lagoon. A city had existed in that spot for more than a thousand years, ruled by an elected Doge and a Council of Ten, chosen from the nobility. For centuries, Venice had been the most prosperous city in Europe, due to its strategic position at the head of the Adriatic Sea and its control of the Mediterranean shipping lanes between the

Byzantine Empire, Persia, and northern Europe (Brown 1997, p. 9). In Venice, Basile would have heard many tales brought by sailors and merchants from faraway lands, including—quite possibly—the Persian love story of Zal and Rudâbeh.

As well as being the hub of world mercantile trade, Venice was also the centre of the European publishing industry. Aldus Manutius had founded the Aldine Press there in 1494, printing the works of Plato, Aristotle, Ovid, and other Greek and Latin classics. His publishing house published small, inexpensive books bound in vellum that could be carried about in a saddlebag or satchel, and read anywhere at any time (Chamberlin 1982, pp. 147-148). These 'Aldine Editions' resulted in the popular dissemination of many old myths and legends throughout Europe, and are highly likely to have been read by Basile during his term as a Venetian soldier. The story of 'Danaë and the Golden Shower' was certainly well-known in Renaissance Venice, for the Venetian artist Tiziano Vecelli (better known as Titian) painted the Greek myth five times between 1544 and 1556 (Goffen 1997, pp. 215-25).

It is also possible Basile heard or read the Jewish tale of 'The Princess in the Tower', as there were many Jews in Venice at that time, and—despite, from 1516, their confinement at night within the confines of the Ghetto—the publishing of Jewish texts flourished under the direction of Daniel

Blomberg and other owners of printing presses (Davis & Ravid 2011, p. 169). In 1553, Pope Julius II ordered the destruction of the Talmud, and many Jewish texts were burned in Piazza San Marco. However, the printing of Hebrew books continued covertly until the interdiction was lifted in the mid-16th century. Certainly Basile—a man interested in old tales—would have had ample opportunity to listen to stories told by a Jewish *maggid*, as the Ghetto at that time was a curiosity that drew many visitors from Venice and elsewhere (Davis & Ravid 2011, pp. x-xix). As a Roman Catholic, Basile would have been familiar with the story of Saint Barbara—it was claimed her bones lay in a chapel on the Venetian island of Murano for centuries. Venetian churches were filled with images of her life and martyrdom, including the famous polyptych painted by the Venetian artist Palma Vecchio in the church of Santa Maria Formosa in 1524 (Doody 2007, p. 243).

From Venice, Basile travelled to Crete (then called Candia), where he served under the Venetian nobleman Andrea Cornaro, who invited him to join the Accademia degli Stravaganti. It is conjectured that he may have begun work on *The Tale Of Tales* at this time (Rak, quoted Canepa 1999, p. 27). In 1608, Basile returned to Naples, where he took up a position at the court of Luigi Carafa, prince of Stigliano, writing songs, plays and poetry for his patron. For the next few years he moved from court to court, taking up positions at Mantua, Montemarano, Zuncoli, Avellion, and elsewhere, using his writing skills to scratch out a living at the various princely courts. In 1631, Mount Vesuvius erupted, and this disaster was followed by a severe outbreak of influenza. Basile died of its effects on 23 February 1632. His sister Adriana arranged the posthumous publication of a number of his writings, including *The Tale of Tales,* between 1634 and 1636. Its ribald vitality and sheer inventiveness ensured its survival when most of Basile's other writings faded away into obscurity (Canepa 1999, pp. 33-34).

The Tale of Tales was a collection of fifty tales, framed by the story of a princess who could not laugh. Various storytellers gather to tell her stories in the hope they can amuse her. One old crone tells the story of a girl named Petrosinella, which begins: 'Once upon a time there was a pregnant woman named Pascadozia, who leaned out of a window overlooking the garden of an ogress and she saw a beautiful bed of parsley. All at once she had such a craving to have some of the parsley she felt she would faint' (Zipes 2001, p. 475).

Basile wrote his fairy tales in the Neapolitan dialect, and so he used the local word 'uerco'. This was later translated into the Italian 'orca', generally translated as ogre. In Nancy L. Canepa's examination of Giambattista Basile's tales, *From Court to Forest,* she devotes a whole chapter to

'Significant Others: Ogres, Fools and Forests.' Ogres, she believes, 'have their most distant origins in the classical underworld deity Orcus… (and) are imagined as savage monsters that devour humans—in particular children' (1999, p. 176). I make reference to this in order to highlight the danger of stealing parsley from an ogress's garden and the vulnerability of any child given up to such a cannibalistic creature. It also seems possible to me that, implicit in Pascadozia's sudden and dangerous craving, the ogress's magic was at work, setting a snare for her.

Nonetheless, Pascadozia steals the parsley and continues to steal until she is inevitably caught by the ogress. She tries to excuse herself by saying she fears her baby will be disfigured by a parsley-shaped birthmark on her face if she does not satisfy her cravings. This is a well-known Italian superstition: a pregnant mother must always be given what she craves, else her thwarted desires could mark the baby (Mazzoni, Zipes and others). The ogress then threatens her until Pascadozia agrees to give up her baby. When the little girl is born, she has a birthmark shaped like a fine sprig of parsley on her breast. So she is named Petrosinella, which means 'little parsley', both for the blemish and for the stolen plant. When the little girl turns seven, the ogress begins to dog her steps, saying, 'Tell your mother to remember her promise.' Eventually the mother cries: 'Take her!'

and so the ogress does, seizing Petrosinella by the hair (Zipes 2001, p. 476).

The ogress locks her up in a tower in the forest, which has 'neither doors nor stairs but only a little window', a phrase with strong echoes of that used in the 8th century Jewish tale, 'The Princess in the Tower'. It was through this window that the ogress climbed in and out of the tower, using Petrosinella's long hair—'and it was very long hair indeed' (p. 476). Petrosinella's hair is described as 'golden banners', and the prince falls in love with her when she sticks her head out of the window and lets her hair down to be bleached by the sun (p. 476). Bleaching one's hair in the sun was common practice for women in Renaissance Venice, where hair of a red-gold colour was highly prized. The Venetian artist Tiziano Vecelli painted women with this red-golden hair colour so often the shade is now called Titian (Cooper 1971, p. 75).

Petrosinella and the prince flirt and eventually make an assignation, the girl giving the ogress a narcotic so that she will sleep. After Petrosinella pulls the prince up by her long braid of hair, he makes 'a little meal out of the saucy parsley of love,' a reference to the parsley-shaped birthmark on her breast. A few lines later, the prince descends by 'the same ladder of gold' (Zipes 2001, p. 476). The prince returns to the tower many times, till the lovers are betrayed by a nosy neighbour who informs the ogress about their liaisons. The ogress tells her neighbour that it is impossible for the maiden to escape as she is bound by a spell. Her only chance of escape is to find and use three magical acorns hidden in the beam of the kitchen.

Petrosinella overhears the ogress's comment and, when the prince comes that night, steals the acorns and makes a ladder out of rope so she and the prince can escape. The ogress is woken by her neighbour's call of alarm, however, and chases after the lovers. Petrosinella throws the acorns over her shoulder, one by one. The first transforms into a ravenous hound, the second into a ferocious lion, and the third into a wolf that devours the ogress. In this way, the ogress is defeated and killed, the heroine Petrosinella gaining access to—and learning to use—the witch's own magical powers in order to triumph over her.

'Petrosinella' is a joyous, bawdy romp, filled with sexual innuendo and a baroque playfulness with language. It is also, most definitely, a story about feminine power: Pascadozia the mother, the ogress (a sinister and liminal figure), and Petrosinella the daughter are the key characters and, although the mother must submit to the ogress and give up her daughter, the girl herself outwits and escapes the ogress.

The south of Italy, Naples and Sicily, were treasure chests of oral storytelling (Zipes 2012, p. 168). On his travels Basile is likely to have heard many tales of witches, goddesses, hags and great mothers and daughters. As Robert Darnton has written, oral storytelling traditions often survive in remarkably stable forms throughout long periods of history, even after the onset of widespread literacy (1985, pp. 16-20). Certainly, the triad of maiden/mother/crone, believed by Göttner-Abendroth to be a remnant of pre-literate matriarchal myths, seems embodied in Basile's tale in a way that was not in earlier Maiden in the Tower tales.

'Petrosinella' would in turn inspire a number of variants which were collected in the Mediterranean area in the late 19th century, including 'Fair Angiola', collected in 1885 by Laura Gonzenbach from Sicily, and 'Anthousa the Fair with the Golden Hair', first recorded in Thrace, Greece, in 1890 (Heiner 2010). Both of these tales include the motif of three magical obstacles and the devouring of the ogress.

There are a number of interesting disparities in these Sicilian and Greek tales. 'Fair Angiola' is the closest to Basile's tale, following much the same sequence of events, except that it is jujubes, or red dates, which are stolen from the witch's garden, not parsley. One detail in particular interested me. When Angiola is seven years of age, the witch approaches her in the street and tells her to inform her mother that it is time to give her up. After the third failed approach, the witch bites off the top of the girl's finger. 'Angiola went home in tears and showed her mother her finger. "Ah!" thought her mother, "there is no help for it. I must give my poor child to the witch, or else she will eat her up in her anger"' (Heiner 2010, p. 15). This is truly a representation of the witch as devouring mother.

The three magical obstacles in 'Fair Angiola' are also different. Instead of acorns, the maiden takes three magic balls of yarn and they are transformed into soap, nails, and finally a river. The witch is not eaten, or killed, but lives to curse Angiola with the face of a dog. In the end, however, the witch relents and gives Angiola some magic water to restore her beauty, so she and the prince may marry.

The Greek variant, 'Anthousa the Fair with the Golden Hair' begins with the prince knocking over the witch's pot of soup, and so she curses him to crave Anthousa as much as she craved soup. The prince searches for the maiden in the tower and persuades her to flee with him. Anthousa takes three magical objects—two combs and a scarf—which are then transformed, one by one, into a swamp, a hedge of thorns, and a sea. Once again the witch is not killed but only delayed, and in the end she too is moved to mercy and helps Anthousa win her prince.

Basile's story was an inspirational force upon my own creative reinterpretation of 'Rapunzel' in a number of significant ways. As stated in my

Introduction, I read about Basile's life and work very early on in the planning process of my novel *Bitter Greens* and was immediately inspired by the possibility of a Venetian setting. I have always been fascinated by Venice and had read many books, both fiction and non-fiction, set in that beautiful but doomed city.

Basile's story also gave me the time of my setting—the 16th century—a period which I have always found interesting. The story told from the point of view of my witch Selena begins in 1504 and moves through to 1582. Margherita's story begins in 1590 and ends in 1600. It was a tumultuous period in Venetian history, with war, plots against the Pope, witchcraft hunts, castration of boy singers, and outbreaks of plague all providing me with ample material to build what I hope was a compelling and suspenseful plot.

It was at this stage of my creative journey that I named my novel *Bitter Greens*. It is named for the parsley that the pregnant woman steals from the ogress's walled garden at the start of Basile's story, the parsley that the girl is named for and which marks her breast. By choosing this title I wanted, somehow, to capture the dynamic and dualistic nature of the ancient vegetative myths I had discovered buried deep within the fairy tale of 'Rapunzel'.

Parsley is a symbolically significant plant, as rich in allusion as an apple or a rose. Its Latin name, *petroselinum crispum*, is derived from the Greek word 'petros' which means 'stone,' referring to the way the plant grows in stony places, and 'selinon', the ancient Greek word for parsley. It is from this formal Latin that the heroine's name 'Petrosinella' is coined in Basile's story. Parsley has long been associated with death and sorrow, according to *The Dictionary of Plant Lore* (Watts 2007, p. 286). Legend says the plant first sprouted in the blood of Archemorus, the old fertility king, whose very name means 'forerunner of death'. Wreaths of parsley were laid on Grecian tombs, and the expression 'to need only parsley' was a euphemistic expression that meant someone was only a step away from death. The Romans dedicated the herb to Persephone and to funeral rites, with wreaths being placed on tombs. Early Christians consecrated it to Saint Peter, guardian of the gates of heaven. In medieval times, it was believed that it was unlucky to transplant parsley, with sayings such as 'plant parsley, plant sorrow' persisting for many years.

Parsley's long association with death led naturally to an association with evil. For example, virgins could not plant it without risking impregnation by the Devil, and its slow germination was because the seeds had to travel to hell and back two, three, seven, or nine times (depending on sources) before they could grow. In *Bitter Greens,* the old nun Seraphina tells

Charlotte-Rose that they were the only two women in the convent who could safely plant parsley seeds, thus intimating that she, like Charlotte-Rose, is not a virgin.

Parsley was also associated with sexuality and fertility. The Greek physician Dioscorides said parsley 'provokes venery and bodily lust', and in Spain it is fed to sheep to bring them into heat. In parts of England, parsley wine was drunk as an aphrodisiac and the phrase 'curly parsley' was once used as a euphemism for pubic hair (Albertson & Albertson 2002, p. 227). Another old saying is 'sow parsley, sow babies', and it was believed that a garden in which parsley refused to grow was a sign of barrenness in the house (Watts 2007, p. 286). Parsley contains the compound apiole, a uterine stimulant, and so the herb was an abortifacient if taken in the early stages of pregnancy, but would be given by midwives to hasten along a slow and difficult labour (Duke 1996).

In *Bitter Greens*, my witch-figure Selena teaches Margherita's mother Pascalina how to make a love spell using parsley to seduce Margherita's father Alessandro and convince him to marry her. Later, when Pascalina is pregnant, she is overcome with an insatiable longing to eat more of the witch's parsley. 'I must eat some or I shall die,' she says (p. 101). The midwife tells Alessandro that he must give Pascalina what she craves, otherwise her thwarted desires will mark the baby. When Margherita is born, she has a parsley-shaped birthmark on her breast. This last detail is one which appears only in Basile's version of the tale.

Another element that I used from Basile's story, which does not occur in any other versions, is the age the child is taken from her parents. In Basile, Petrosinella is taken by the ogress at the age of seven; in later renderings of the tale, the child is taken at birth. My heroine Margherita is also taken from home at the age of seven. I decided to do this firstly because I wished my character Margherita to have happy memories of her home and parents and, secondly, so she would be aware she had been kidnapped and long to return to her family. Margherita is sent to the foundling hospital and musical academy, the Ospedale della Pietà, in Venice, where she would be taught to sing. Although the heroine does not sing in Basile's version of the tale, she does in La Force's version and so in nearly all later versions. In *Bitter Greens* Margherita is re-named Petrosinella by the witch, and is called by that name thereafter. However, she refuses to accept the false name and makes for herself a mantra in which she tells herself, 'Her name was Margherita. Her parents had loved her. One day, she would escape.'

At twelve, Margherita is taken from the Ospedale and locked up in a tower on a peninsula jutting out into a deep lake. This edifice is based on a real-life tower at Manerba de Garda, a small town on Lake Garda in northern Italy. In Renaissance times, a tower was built there on the site of a shrine to Minerva, Roman goddess of wisdom and war. Thorns still grow around its ruins. It took me a long time to find the right place for my imaginary tower, yet when I read about the tower at Manerba, it felt as if it was meant to be. I very much wanted to connect Margherita to the ideal of ancient feminine wisdom embodied by Minerva.

It is Basile who first gave his heroine the extraordinarily long golden hair which was to become the most recognised visual symbol of 'Rapunzel' tales. In some stories and illustrations, the girl's hair is yellow; in others, it is a vivid red-gold. I always knew my Rapunzel would have the latter and, indeed, a startling large number of my fictional heroines have long red hair. Red is the colour of blood and fire and the rising full moon, and so symbolises the forces of life, love, passion, and fertility. It is also the colour of the Mother Goddess's cloak in Göttner-Abendroth's theory of matriarchal myths.

In *Bitter Greens,* both my witch-figure Selena and my maiden-figure Margherita have golden-red hair, and it is the vibrant colour of her hair that draws the former to the latter. The intensity of Selena's attraction to red hair could be seen as fetishistic. As Wendy Cooper has written, of all the hair colours, red is the one that can excite the most extreme reactions, 'perhaps (because of) the legend that red-haired women are especially passionate', with redheaded women in the 16th and 17th centuries often put to death on suspicion of witchcraft (1971, p. 71).

One of my biggest problems in re-writing 'Rapunzel' as a historical novel was how to explain the impossibly long hair without the escape hatch of magic. Most retellings do not bother to explain or show this unnatural growth; those that do simply say it was due to the witch's sorcery. I had to find another explanation. In *Bitter Greens* Margherita has the hair of eight dead girls—former prisoners of the tower—sewn into her hair by the witch Selena.

Later in the story, Margherita seeks to find a way to escape her imprisonment. Her tower room, like the one in Basile's story, had no visible door or stair. Margherita is sure there must be another way out, however. Finding a trapdoor hidden under the carpet of her tower room, Margherita spends days chipping away at the stone until she can raise the trapdoor, and descend the steps hidden below into darkness. Hidden far below, in the cellar, she finds the skeletons of eight dead girls. One of the skeletons has, 'a thick hank of filthy, matted hair coiling in the cavity below her ribs'. This girl would have been suffering from trichophagia, which is the compulsive eating of one's own hair. It is an impulse control disorder associated with trichotillomania, or the pulling out of one's own hair, and is normally caused by intense anxiety and stress. Trichophagia is often called 'Rapunzel syndrome' and, since hair is indigestible, can lead to death (Frey *et al* 2005, p. 9). It seemed to me quite likely that a girl kept locked away in a tower for years may well develop an anxiety disorder centred on hair, particularly when her captor had trichophilia (hair fetishism).

Another compelling detail of Basile's tale was that his heroine was bound to her tower by a spell, and could not escape until she learned to use the ogress's own magic against her. I had always been troubled by the heroine's inability to escape her tower earlier, and this seemed to be a very likely and powerful reason for her not to simply climb down a rope brought to her by the prince. Margherita not only needs to learn to use the witch's magic, but also to overcome her own paralysing fear and sense of powerlessness.

A key motif that I borrowed from Basile—and also from the Sicilian and Greek variants—was that of the three magical objects that transformed into obstacles in the path of the witch. However, I did not use Petrosinella's three acorns, but rather ones inspired by the Greek tale 'Anthousa the Fair with the Golden Hair'. The heroine in that tale stole two combs and a scarf from the witch. When she threw them over her shoulder, they were transformed into a swamp, a hedge of thorns, and the sea. I felt that the use of tools normally used in the control and confinement of hair was symbolically more powerful than the use of acorns (as powerful as these are). So my maiden Margherita threw a hair-snood made of silver thread which transformed into a net to entrap the witch; a ribbon which changed into a thick rope so that she could climb out the tower window; and a comb which turned into the thicket of thorns about the tower base which later blinded the young prince, Lucio. In this way, Margherita overcomes the witch by using her own magic against her, just as Petrosinella did in Basile's tale.

Another detail which I borrowed from the Basile variants is the device of the witch biting off the top of the little girl's finger, which appears in the Sicilian tale, 'Fair Angiola'. I wanted the effect of emotional shock and surprise that this would cause the reader, and also to destabilise their expectations. This was not 'Rapunzel' as they knew it.

Finally, Giambattista Basile himself appears as a minor character in *Bitter Greens*, in the final section of Margherita's story. He meets my heroine and hero after their final confrontation with Selena. In that chance meeting, Giambattista (named by his first name here to distinguish the fictional man from the real man) expresses his desire to write stories but admits unhappily that he must go to Venice to work as a soldier instead, due to his lack of funds. Margherita and her prince Lucio share their story with him (thereby explaining how he could come to know the tale), and he disapproves of the ending. Giambattista thinks the witch should have been killed which is, of course, what happens in his version of the tale.

In Basile's story, desire is the engine which drives the plot. The mother's craving for parsley, the ogress's wish for the child, the prince's lust for the imprisoned maiden, and her longing to be free. I see this sensuality as a blossoming of the story's deeply buried roots in the ancient fertility religion of the Great Goddess, and so my novel *Bitter Greens* is also filled with yearnings and desires of all kinds.

Chapter 4

Healing Tears: Charlotte-Rose de La Force & Persinette

In 1697, sixty-four years after the posthumous publication of 'Petrosinella', the French noblewoman Charlotte-Rose de Caumont de La Force published her own collection of fairy tales, named—like Basile's collection—*The Tale of Tales* (*Contes Des Contes*). This collection included La Force's Maiden in the Tower tale, 'Persinette'.

La Force was born into an aristocratic family in 1650, the younger of two sisters. Her father—who died when she was only a baby—was the seventh son of the Duc de La Force, a proud and fervent Huguenot who had fought against the king in the bloody religious wars of the early 17th century. Her mother was King Louis XIV's second cousin and the chatelaine of a medieval castle in Gascony, the Château de Cazeneuve (Souloumiac 2004, p. 35-37).

Situated about twenty-five miles south of Bordeaux, on the pilgrim's road that ran from Santiago de Compostela to Vézelay, the Château de Cazeneuve had been constructed as a fortress in the early 14th century by the Duc d'Albret. Its thirteen outer walls were built high and strong about an inner courtyard, with two cone-topped Rapunzel-like towers at the front (p. 34). In the 16th century, the château was used as a hunting lodge by the young Huguenot king, Henri III of Navarre. His marriage to the French Catholic princess Marguerite de Valois (known to history as Queen Margot) sparked the bloody St Bartholomew's Day massacres in August 1573 in which thousands of French Protestants died. Their marriage was unhappy and King Henri later incarcerated his wife, Queen Margot, in a series of strongholds for eighteen years, including at the Château de Cazeneuve. Growing up there seventy-odd years later, La Force would have been very familiar with the stories of the imprisoned queen and her struggles to live a self-determined life. Every day she would have seen the quotation Queen Margot had engraved on the drawing room mantlepiece: 'Beauty is in the eye of the beholder, and a prison will never be a place of beauty' (p. 36).

Growing up in south-west France, La Force would have been steeped in the troubadour tradition of Aquitaine, with its poems and songs and stories of medieval romance. La Force would also have read tales from the famous *Bibliothèque Bleue*, booklets of stories covered in cheap blue-grey wrappers that were carried around by peddlers in their sacks. Many of these stories were translations of obscure medieval *chansons de geste*, and other tales of bold derring-do (Thelander 1982, pp. 467-

496; Darnton 1985, p. 63). It is therefore most likely that La Force would have known the story of Floris and Blanchefleur, though she may not—being Protestant—have known that of St Barbara and her tower.

When La Force was ten years old, the royal court came to stay at the Château de Cazeneuve for a few nights. His Most Catholic Majesty King Louis XIV was on his way to Spain to meet his new wife, the Infanta Maria Theresa of Spain. Two years later, La Force's mother, the Baroness of Cazeneuve, was forcibly taken from the château and incarcerated in a convent, even though she was a devout Huguenot. She was to be imprisoned until she recanted her faith and was baptised as a Catholic. Since she died in the convent, it seems she refused. La Force and her elder sister Marie became wards of the king (Souloumiac 2004, pp. 39-40).

At the age of sixteen, La Force was summoned to court to serve as one of Queen Marie-Therese's ladies-in-waiting. She scandalised the court with her wayward behaviour, first taking as her lover Molière's protégé, the actor Michel Baron, and then becoming engaged to the Marquis of Nesle. It was whispered that La Force had ensnared the marquis with black magic. She was eventually called before the *Chambre Ardente*, the French Inquisition, and questioned, but no charges were laid. The French court was at that time convulsed by the Affair of the Poisons, a scandal about poison, murder,

Satanism and infanticide which had implicated the king's favourite mistress. Whether it was La Force's kinship with the king, or whether the king feared what further investigations would reveal about those closest to him, can never be known, but La Force was lucky not be burned at the stake like many other women at that time (p. 41).

Then La Force fell in love with a much younger man, Charles Briou. When his family kidnapped him and locked him up in their château, La Force disguised herself in a bearskin and visited with a travelling troupe of actors. Hidden in the guise of a dancing bear, she was able to speak with her lover and make a plan for his release. As soon as he was free, the couple eloped and for ten days were blissfully happy. Then Briou's father had La Force charged with unlawfully marrying a minor (even though they married a month after he had turned twenty-five, the legal age of consent), and the court found in his favour. The marriage was annulled and La Force was charged a thousand gold *louis (p.* 41).

Desperately poor, La Force turned her hand to writing. She had always been an active figure in the Parisian literary salons of the late 17th century, being one of the earliest *conteuses,* or female fairy tale tellers, along with the Baroness d'Aulnoy, Madame de Murat, and Mademoiselle L'Héritier. It was here that the craze for fairy tales began, with participants being called upon to 'invent' and tell tales on the spot (Harries 2001, p. 61).

La Force also wrote a series of 'secret histories'—historical novels that told the 'true' story of people such as the scandalous Queen Margot, published as *Histoire de Marguerite de Valois, reine de Navarre* in 1696. Her books were enormously popular, although most had to be published outside France to escape the king's censors. Rumours that she had become the Dauphin's mistress, and the publication of some satirical Christmas carols, displeased the ageing and now fanatically devout king, and La Force was given the choice of exile or the convent. Although she was born a Huguenot, La Force had already abjured and converted to Catholicism after the Revocation of the Edict of Nantes in 1685 outlawed Protestantism. La Force therefore chose the convent, and spent the next eleven years locked inside its high, stone walls. While there, she wrote her collection of fairy tales, which was published in 1697, the same year as Charles Perrault's *Tales from Mother Goose* and the Baroness d'Aulnoy's *Tales of Fairies* (Souloumiac 2004, pp. 41-42).

Unlike Perrault's tales, d'Aulnoy and La Force's tales were sophisticated, complex, and self-consciously literary. Elizabeth Wanning Harries believes such tales 'are complex in their reimaginings of well-known and more conventional fairy-tale patterns and motifs.' (2003, pp. 16-17) Two-thirds of all the fairy tales written and published in France between 1690 and 1715 were written by just seven women, including d'Aulnoy, La Force, La Force's cousin Henriette-Julie de Murat, Perrault's niece Marie-Jeanne L'Héritier de Villandon, and Catherine Bernard, who said of the *conte de fees*: 'the (adventures) should always be implausible and the emotions always natural' (Harries 2003, p. 35).

La Force's fairy tales, published under the pseudonym "Mademoiselle de X", proved very popular. The money she earned through her writing, plus her growing literary reputation, at last secured her freedom, but she was not permitted to return to court. She moved to Paris and was an active figure in the literary salons until her death in 1724, aged seventy-four (Souloumiac 2004, p. 44).

In La Force's tale 'Persinette'[8], a pregnant woman longs for some parsley, but it is such a rare plant that it grows only in a fairy's beautiful garden. The woman's husband, troubled by her longing, walks along the walls of the garden day and night trying to find a way to climb over. One day, he finds the gate to the garden open and steals a handful of parsley, which his wife eats hungrily. The wife's desire for parsley only grows, however, and her young husband again seeks to steal some for her. Again he finds the gate open, but this time he is caught by the fairy. She tells him that he can have as much parsley as he likes if he will give her the child once it is born. Taken from her parents at birth, the child is named Persinette, a name coined from the French word *persil* meaning 'parsley'.

As in Basile's story, the symbolic linkage between child and plant is clear.

Persinette is locked up in a silver tower in the middle of the forest at the age of twelve. Although she has every luxury, the young woman is lonely and sings to amuse herself. A young prince hears her and falls in love with her. Overhearing the fairy's command, 'Persinette, let down your hair so I can climb up', the prince calls out the chant and the maiden lowers her golden hair to him. He climbs up and jumps into her chamber, where he bows down before Persinette 'and embraced her knees with an ardour that was to persuade her of his love'. Persinette's heart is 'full of all the love she could possibly feel for this prince'.

In a short time, Persinette falls pregnant but, due to her naivety, has no idea what her sickness means. The fairy however, recognises 'the malady'. She cuts off Persinette's braid, casts her out into the forest, then— invoking her power—she causes the prince to throw himself from the top of the tower. He is blinded by thorns and wanders about in desperation, groaning Persinette's name. Some years pass. At last he hears the sound of a familiar voice singing. He finds Persinette and her twin children, more beautiful than the day is bright, to whom she has given birth while alone in the forest. Persinette weeps with joy. 'But what a miracle! No sooner had her precious tears fallen on the prince's eyes than he regained his full vision'.

However, when Persinette and the prince try to eat, all their food turns to stone and their water to crystals. Herbs turn into toads and venomous snakes, 'birds became dragons and vixens flew around them, glaring at them in a terrifying way'. Clutching their children in their arms, the couple prepare themselves to die. The fairy is, at last, moved to mercy by their unwavering love and courage. She transports them to safety at the king's palace where they are greeted with delight, and 'nothing in the world could be compared to the happiness in which (the prince) lived with his perfect wife'.

La Force's tale 'Persinette' (1697) was therefore the first in which the complete 'Rapunzel' memeplex appears: the theft of the forbidden food, the surrendering of the child, the woman of mysterious magical powers, the maiden, the tower, the hair-ladder, the prince, the birth of twins, the healing tears, and the redemption of the captor through her final mercy to her captives. No other variant of the tale culminates in this way. As Getty has written: 'Mlle de La Force's ending…was her own unique creation' (1997, p. 39).

La Force's changes to the story have a profound impact upon the development of the heroine's agency. In 'Persinette', the young woman sings 'in the most extraordinary way' to comfort herself in her loneliness and so draws the prince towards her. Although she betrays herself in her innocence, when Persinette is banished to the wilderness, she bears twins alone, without help, and cares for them alone, without help. Persinette heals the prince's blinded eyes with her tears, and then prevails upon the fairy to forgive and help them, and so is responsible for the fairy's redemption as well as her own salvation. It was La Force's version of the tale which spoke to me most powerfully—both as a child imprisoned by illness caused by my own inability to control my tears, and as an adult searching to make sense of this fairy tale that had haunted me for so many years.

The method by which La Force came to know Basile's story 'Petrosinella' is a mystery. The story had not yet been translated into either Italian or French, and was not widely known outside Naples where it was published. The fairy tale scholar Suzanne Magnanini has found a number of possible routes by which Basile's stories could have arrived in France in the 1680s. A French printer working in Naples, Antonio Bulifon, had printed an edition of *Lo cunto de li cunti* in 1674. It is possible that a copy was purchased from him by the Benedictine monk, Jean Mabillon, in 1685 while on a book-buying mission for the French king. Otherwise, Bulifon may have brought a copy of the tales to France himself when he returned to France in 1687 (Magnanini, pp. 78-92).

Zipes has argued that oral sources are the primary explanation for the explosion of fairy tales in France in the 1690s. Many of the *conteuses* such as d'Aulnoy and La Force make reference to nannies and servants who told them tales; he also believes that it is highly unlikely that the French fairy tale retellers could decipher Basile's difficult Neapolitan dialect (2012, pp. 166-167). However, I think it worth remembering that La Force, like most aristocratic Huguenot women of her time, was extremely well-educated. It is likely she could read both Latin and Italian. The Neapolitan dialect, when written, shows some key resemblances to both of these languages (Galiani, quoted in Bottigheimer 2012, p. 89).

There were many Italians at the French royal court in the late 1600s, including the family of Cardinal Mazarin, who was born in Naples in 1602 and acted as the French chief minister until his death in 1661. His seven nieces, known collectively as the Mazarinettes, were all born and grew to young adulthood in Italy. They were brought to Paris by their uncle and became well-known figures in the court life of the late 17th century, marrying into many important aristocratic families. La Force would have known the Mazarinettes well in her role as maid-of-honour to the queen, particularly Olympe Mancini, the second eldest of the Mazarinettes, who was superintendent of the Queen's household (Fraser 2006, pp. 36-37). In addition, most Italians at the time were familiar with the Neapolitan dialect because of its use in theatre and *commedia dell'arte* (Canepa 1999, p. 64).

It is therefore entirely possible that a group of *conteuses*—La Force among them—found a book of bawdy Italian fairy tales and managed to translate some, if not all, of the stories. Perhaps the reason why the first half of La Force's 'Persinette' is so similar to Basile's 'Petrosinella', but the second half so different, is simply because she only managed to translate the first few pages before her patience, her eyesight, or her willingness to decipher the dense and difficult dialect ran out. I, however, think it far more likely that La Force simply took from Basile's tale the motifs and plot points that spoke to her most powerfully, and rewrote the end to please herself. In *Bitter Greens* I solve the mystery quite differently. Charlotte-Rose hears the story of the girl in the tower from the old nun, Sœur Seraphina, who is, as it is revealed at the end of the book, intimately involved in the circumstances herself. In this revelation, the three narrative strands are tied together in an unexpected and surprising way (or so I hope).

La Force's first significant change to Basile's tale was to transform the antagonist from an ogress, a hideous cannibalistic creature, into a fairy, something at once more mysterious and more benign. As Marina Warner has described in *From the Beast to the Blonde*, the word 'fairy' has its roots in the Latin word 'fata' which refers to a goddess of destiny: 'fairies share with Sibyls knowledge of the future and the past, and...foretell events to come and give warnings' (1994, pp. 14-15).

Basile never gave his ogress a motive for locking away Petrosinella. La Force, however, says, 'Before Persinette reached the age of twelve, she was a marvel to behold, and since the fairy was fully aware of what fate had in store for her, she decided to shield her from her destiny' (Zipes 2001, p. 480). The tower in which Persinette is locked away is silver, and therefore symbolic of the moon. It is furnished splendidly with all a girl could ever want. As in 'Petrosinella', the prince comes and seduces Persinette, but from that point on the story departs from Basile's version. Persinette betrays herself by not realising that her 'maladie' is in fact pregnancy, the fairy cuts off her 'precious braids', and Persinette is cast out into the wilderness, bears twins by herself, and in time finds the prince and heals his blinded eyes (pp. 482-483). However, the family is still lost and starving. In La Force's tale, the fairy is moved by their plight and takes pity upon them, magically restoring them to the prince's family. In this way the fairy herself is redeemed.

Annabel Patterson has written: 'Interpreted by specific cultures yet relevant throughout the ages, the fable speaks...in metaphoric codes that can emancipate both the teller and listener...Fables tell us that we have choices to make' (quoted in

Zipes 2012, p. 13). Scholars such as Dundes and Zipes contend that this is also true of fairy tales and other types of folklore such as songs, nursery rhymes, and legends (Dundes 1980, pp. 33-40; Zipes 2012, pp. 17-20). Fairy tales therefore gain much of their power from the way their motifs become metaphoric codes, carrying hidden meanings that can empower both teller and listener. La Force was born in Gascony, which has a long tradition of travelling troubadours who carried news and subversive views concealed in songs or fables or folk tales (Goffman & Joy 2007, p. 123). She would have been acutely aware of the ways in which her tale would be read by the king and the court.

I believe it is possible that, in La Force's story, the tower stood for the convent in which she was incarcerated and the figure of the fairy, the girl's captor, was a representation of the king, on whose order La Force was imprisoned. This explains why the captor was no longer a hungry ogress but instead a wise and protective fairy, and why La Force lavished so much time on describing her kindness and thoughtfulness. Persinette angered the fairy by her disobedience—as La Force had angered the king—but in the end, the fairy took pity on her and restored her to the life of the court, as La Force herself no doubt wished to be restored.

La Force may also have deliberately drawn upon the symbols and narrative structures of pre-literate goddess myths which endured in the rich Gascon folklore of her childhood. The Aquitaine area is rich in evidence of such gynocentric myths. One striking example is an ancient lead tablet found near Larzac, a town a few hours east of Préchac where La Force grew up. Dated to 90 BC, the tablet depicts women performing a secret ritual and is inscribed: 'Behold the magic of women, their special underworld names, the prophecy of the seer who weaves this magic' (Monaghan 2009, p. 295). Many Palaeolithic stone sculptures and bas-relief carvings depicting voluptuous female figures have also been found in Aquitaine and the Pyrénées—more so than in any other part of the world (Dixson & Dixson 2011).

La Force may have chosen to change the character of the girl's captor from the cannibalistic monster in Basile's tale to a wise Sybil, a goddess of destiny, in order to deliberately link the story back to older gynocentric myths that celebrate all aspects of feminine power. In these tales, the older woman embodies the third face of the Great Goddess and is an agent of the forces of transformation that bring about rebirth and regeneration.

La Force's crone keeps the maiden safe in a silver tower (a symbol of the moon) until the time for growth and change has arrived. She tests both the maiden and the hero, then—when the time is ripe—cuts the maiden free so she can be reborn into the world and become a mother of twin babies, a boy and a girl. Like Apollo and Artemis, they embody the dualistic nature of the universe, the forces of day and night, light and darkness, sun and moon, masculine and feminine. It is by the crone's actions that the maiden reaches her full potential in the world, as an agent of liberation, healing and redemption, and the hero fulfils his role in the sacred marriage that keeps the wheel of life and death and rebirth turning. In La Force's tale, the crone therefore regained her original role as the harbinger of change and growth, a 'midwife to the psyche' (Caputi, in Larrington 1992, p. 433).

La Force's motifs of wounding and healing, darkness and light, sacrifice and redemption, were most likely introduced in the full knowledge of their ancient symbolic meaning. As Harries says in *Twice Upon A Time: Women Writers and the History of the Fairy Tale*, 'the *conteuses* (were)... knowing, educated, worldly-wise...with a wry and sometimes sardonic view of the narrative constellations they are reusing and revising... (their) complex tales work to reveal the stories behind other stories, the unvoiced possibilities that tell a different tale' (2001, pp. 15-17).

It was these metaphoric codes in La Force's tale, preserved in the Grimm Brothers' version, which first drew me to the story now known as 'Rapunzel'. It was La Force's steadfast refusal to conform to the strict patriarchal norms of 17th century French society that drew me to want to tell her life story.

La Force's tale 'Persinette' was the first tale in which the witch cuts off the maiden's braid of impossibly long hair, an act which I find symbolically significant. Because hair continually replenishes itself, it has for centuries been imbued with symbolic power. In social-political history, having one's head shaved can be a form of humiliation. Prisoners-of-war often have their hair cropped close to the skull, while French women suspected of being collaborators at the end of the Second World War had their heads shaved against their will (Koppelman 1996, p. 87). The story of Samson and Delilah, and the Norse Goddess Sif (whose glorious golden hair was chopped from her head by the trickster Loki) are just two of many myths associated with the cutting of hair.

In such stories, hair is nearly always associated with strength, power and sexuality; in other words, with the potency of life. Hair is thus linked to the magical thread of life which is spun, measured, and finally severed by the Three Fates of ancient Greek mythology. The witch's scissors are reminiscent of what Milton described as the "abhorred shears" of Atropos, the third of the Fates. As mentioned above, fairies are etymologically and symbolically linked to the Fates, and so the cutting of Persinette's hair by the fairy can be seen to be symbolic of both the loss of her virginity and a kind of metaphoric wounding, or death. However, the cutting of the braid can also be interpreted as the cutting of a symbolic umbilical cord, and Persinette's expulsion from the small tower room as a kind of birth. As discussed earlier, the key psychological drama of gynocentric mythology is that of birth, life, death and rebirth. So the cutting of the maiden's hair symbolically ends one life and begins another. Similarly, the cutting of Charlotte-Rose's hair in the opening chapters of *Bitter Greens* signifies the end of her courtly life and the beginning of a new life in very different circumstances.

As stated previously, La Force's motif of the healing tears was the story element that resonated with me most powerfully and so I was always going to include this as a key scene in my retelling of 'Rapunzel'. It is one of the most strikingly original aspects of La Force's tale. The anthropologist Marija Gimbutas sees tears as being divine: 'the eyes of the goddess are the source of life-sustaining water' (2009, p. 53). Symbolically, tears are linked to life-giving rain and the salty waters of life-endowing amniotic fluids, and to the ocean, cradle of all existence.

In the Bible—which La Force would have been well acquainted with, thanks to her Huguenot upbringing—the prophet Ezekial is horrified at the sight of women 'weeping for Tammuz'. Tammuz was the consort-king of the goddess Ishtar. He had been banished to the underworld and could only be resurrected to life again by the weeping of tears. The ritualistic lament by the priestesses of Ishtar was thus seen as a powerful and sacred ceremony in a pre-Christian fertility rite, which explains Ezekial's revulsion (Nelson 2005).

I therefore find it most striking that La Force chose to use tears as a source of healing and enlightenment in her tale, when she would have been acutely aware of its links to a goddess-worshipping pagan religion. In fact, La Force seems to have shown little piety at a time when questions of religion were causing dissension and war all through France. She abjured the faith of her forefathers when Protestantism was outlawed, unlike many other Huguenots who either died or fled France, and—unlike most of the *conteuses*—her tales are remarkably free of religious expressions.

When using the motif of the healing tears in my own work, I had to think how best to frame this scene plausibly within a historical context while still retaining the beauty and mystery of the scene. In *Bitter Greens*, Lucio's eyes are not put out by the thorns, but glued shut with dried blood from his scratched face. Margherita's tears moisten the crust of dried blood and wash it away, so that he can see the gleam of light through her red-gold hair. Margherita draws the blinded Lucio to her through the darkness of the night by the sound of her singing, just as she earlier drew him to the tower and into love.

This aspect of the tale has always been one that appealed to me—the entrapped girl who sang with all her strength and so summoned the instrument of change and release to her. Whenever I argue in public forums about Rapunzel being perceived as the typical 'passive princess' (which I seem to do quite often), I point out that she was certainly no princess (her parents were so poor they sold her for a handful of bitter greens), and she was certainly not passive. She sings though she can have had little hope of being heard; she pulls the prince up by her hair, giving him ingress to her tower; she allows him to seduce her (there is no suggestion of rape in any of the early versions of 'Rapunzel'; sexual congress is described as both willing and joyful); and, in most versions of the tale, she conspires with him to escape the tower.

Persinette's song is born out of her body and her breath. It is pure emotion expressed in sound. Unlike screaming—which exhausts the physique, rasps the voice, and unsettles and alienates with its raw expression of rage and terror—singing can be sustained over a long period of time and invites empathy and connection. I have always felt that the maiden's singing was an important and beautiful part of the fairy tale, and so I have a strong element of musicality in the novel. Margherita spends time at the Ospedale della Pietà in Venice, where she is taught to sing, and she ends the book singing in the first opera ever performed, Jacopo Peri's *Euridice*.

I also drew on Renaissance musical terms such as cantata, reverie, and interlude as the titles for each section, to highlight the importance of singing and music, which I see as a metaphor for the maiden discovering her own voice, and using that voice to save herself.

As an oral storyteller, I too need to use my voice in order to connect with an audience, to entrance and enchant them, to sway them emotionally and, I hope, to communicate some kind of new understanding. So I felt an affinity with the girl who sings out from her lonely tower room, and I understood why she kept on singing even with no hope of ever being heard. Singing is like storytelling. We tell stories to entertain, to express ourselves, to warn, to teach, and to change the way people think—strong motivations, I believe, for both La Force and myself.

Chapter 5

The Dark Sorceress: Wilhelm Grimm & Rapunzel

Almost a hundred years after La Force wrote 'Persinette', her tale made its way over the Alps and was transformed at last into the tale known as 'Rapunzel'.

Once again, there is no clear path from La Force's story and its 18th century German incarnations, which would find their best-known expression in the Grimm Brothers' collection. La Force's *Contes des Contes* was reprinted in French several times between 1707 and 1725, and then translated into German for the first time by Frederick Immanuel Bierling in 1765, and included in Volume 8 of his collection *Cabinet der Feen* (Bottigheimer 2012, p. 197). A young German writer named Friedrich Schulz then included a version of the tale in the fifth volume of his novel *Kleine Romane*, published in 1790 (Zipes 2001, p. 484). Schulz himself claimed that he had heard the tale from a 'gute Frau', but the story is so close to La Force's most scholars believe he must indeed have read her tale (Getty 1997, p. 40), perhaps during his travels to France in 1789.

Schulz's 'Rapunzel' is a loose translation of La Force's story, and adheres closely to the major plot points. He did, however, make a number of modifications. The most obvious of these is the changing of the maiden's name to 'Rapunzel'. No scholar has been able to definitively explain this name change. It is interesting to conjecture a number of possible reasons. 'Rapunzel' is the common name of *campanula rapunculus*, a wild herb called 'bellflower rampion' in English, and commonly shortened to 'rampion'. The word is derived from *rapa* which means turnip. The roots of rapunzel can be boiled and eaten like parsnips, and the leaves—although bitter—can be used in a winter salad. In spring, the young shoots can be blanched and eaten like asparagus. Nowadays, *campanula rapunculus* is more usually grown for its pretty, blue sprays of flowers (Watts 2007, p. 313). Marina Warner, however, links rapunzel to German rampion, once nicknamed 'kings-cure-all' for its supposed healing properties (2008). Now better known as evening primrose, it is a bright golden plant that certainly reflects the much-vaunted colour of the maiden's hair.

Schulz may have changed the heroine's name because parsley is a Mediterranean plant that grows best in warm, temperate climates, and so may have been relatively unknown in northern Germany, where Schulz was born. Perhaps Rapunzel simply sounded prettier—or as the Swiss fairy tale scholar Max Lüthi has postulated—more forceful in the German tongue. The German translation of 'Persinette' or 'Little Parsley' would be 'Petersilchen'. As Lüthi wrote, 'Rapunzel sounds better in the German tale than Persinette, it has a more forceful sound than *Petersilchen*...To be sure, in folk beliefs the plants called rapunzel do not play any important role, quite in contrast to those...such as parsley and fennel, apples and pears, which are attributed eroticizing and talismanic properties' (quoted in McGlathery 1991, p. 130). It can therefore be seen that the change of the heroine's name to Rapunzel drained much of the symbolic meaning from the herb, and in many cases led to the link between girl and plant being broken.

Two other significant changes in Schulz's version were that the prince is not flung from the tower by the witch, but leaps out himself in a fit of despair, and Rapunzel betrays herself by complaining to the witch that her dress has grown too tight for her (a device I use in *Bitter Greens*, as a sign of the innocent naïvety of the young woman who does not know she is pregnant).

The Grimm brothers included the 'Rapunzel' fairy tale in their first fairy tale collection, *Kinder-und-Hausmärchen*, published in 1812. Jakob Grimm was then twenty-seven years old and his brother Wilhelm a year younger. They had been born in Hanau, in Hessen-Kassel, then a small electorate in the crazy patchwork of countries that made up the Holy Roman Empire of the German nation. The brothers were the eldest of a family of six, with three other boys and a girl born after them. The death of their father in 1796 had changed the lives of the Grimm family profoundly. Their mother was left without any income but a small pension. Her sister, Henriette Zimmer, offered to help with the two eldest boys' education, and so Jakob and Wilhelm went to live in Kassel, where their Aunt Zimmer was a lady-in-waiting to the Electress Wilhelmine.

With the patronage of the Elector, the two young men were admitted to the University of Marburg, studying law. One of their professors, Friedrich von Savigny, inspired them with a love of history and literature. Jakob did not complete his law degree, instead accompanying von Savigny to Paris and returning to Kassel in 1805, determined to find a way to build a career from his love of philology. Wilhelm matriculated from university and returned to Kassel in 1806, the same year that Napoleon's Grand Army invaded the small electorate. The Elector fled, with his family and cartloads of treasures, and the citizens of Hessen-Kassel came under French rule. Napoleon created a new Kingdom of Westphalia by mashing together half-a-dozen small kingdoms, and set his twenty-two year old brother Jerome to rule.

As a small act of defiance against the cultural domination of the French, the Grimm brothers began to collect old folk tales. Initially, they transcribed tales from old books and manuscripts, including 'Rapunzel' from Schulz's *Kleine Romaine*. At this time, the brothers were aiming to keep their stories as close as possible to the original source—whether oral or literary—and so their 'Rapunzel' was similar to Schulz's version, except that, for some reason, Wilhelm omitted the fairy's final act of mercy. She disappears from the story and is not heard of again. Another key change is that La Force's description of the luxuriousness of the fairy's silver tower is not included, making the story both simpler and darker (Heiner 2013, p. 3).

In 1808, Frau Grimm died. Her widow's pension was suspended, and the young members of the family were so poor they could only afford a single meal a day. Meanwhile, Napoleon slowly conquered most of the rest of Europe. The first fairy tale collection was published on December 20, 1812, the same time as news of Napoleon's disastrous march on Moscow became known.

The *Kinder-und-Hausmärchen* was a failure. Only 900 copies sold in the next three years. Even worse, the Grimm Brothers were critically lambasted. One reviewer said the stories were 'the most pathetic and tasteless material imaginable', and several singled out 'Rapunzel' for especial criticism, Friedrich Rühs writing: 'What proper mother or nanny could tell the fairy tale about Rapunzel to an innocent daughter without blushing?' (Tatar 2003, p. 18) In a culture as rule-bound and conservative as the Holy Roman Empire of the German Nations, a tale which derived much of its power from uncontrollable longings and sexual desire was always going to be frowned upon.

In 1819, the Grimm Brothers brought out a new edition of the fairy tales. As Harries has said so vividly, 'those nervous nineteenth century Nellies' reworked many of the stories to make them more palatable to a conservative, middle-class readership (2001, p. 8). In their choice of tales, and in their comprehensive reworking of the language of the tales chosen, the Grimm Brothers served a socialisation process that celebrated the attitudes of the bourgeoisie society in which they lived, one which 'placed great emphasis on passivity, industry and self-sacrifice for girls, and on activity, competition, and the accumulation of wealth for boys' (Zipes 2012, p. 58).

Of the editorial emendations made by Wilhelm Grimm, those to 'Rapunzel' were among the most profound. In the 1819 version Rapunzel betrays herself by remarking that the witch is much heavier to pull up than the prince, rather than by complaining her dress no longer fits her, thereby alerting the witch to her pregnancy. Rapunzel and the prince are 'married' in the tower, and after her banishment into the wilderness, Rapunzel no longer gives birth to twins, though the children continue—rather confusingly—to appear at their parents' reunion in all the ensuing editions. The tale continued to be cut and modified until the Grimms' seventh and final edition in 1857, from which most other retellings of 'Rapunzel' are descended (including Lucy Crane's version, which is the one I read as a child).

As Tatar notes in *The Hard Facts of the Grimms' Fairy Tales*:

> it is easy to leap to the conclusion that Teutonic prudishness or the Grimms' delicate sense of propriety motivated the kinds of changes made in 'Rapunzel'. That may well be the case. But it is far more likely to assume that Wilhelm Grimm took to heart the criticisms levelled against his volume and, eager to find a wider audience, set to work making the appropriate changes. His nervous sensitivity about moral objections to the tales in the collection reflects a growing desire to write for children rather than to collect for scholars (2003, pp. 18-19).

There is no doubt that Wilhelm Grimm's changes to the story drained it of much of its subversive power. Rapunzel is a far less active and appealing character than either Petrosinella or Persinette. Her self-betrayal to the witch makes her seem stupid, and the erotic charge of the Italian and French versions is utterly diluted and made pale and limp (Basile's prince feasts upon the parsley of love, La Force's prince embraces her knees with ardour, but Wilhelm's prince talks to her in a friendly way and takes her hand).

Nonetheless, Wilhelm Grimm made one key change which I find interesting and powerful. He changed La Force's benign fairy into a sorceress, a figure of mighty and fearful magic. The word 'sorceress' comes, through tangled byways, from the Latin *sors* which means 'lot, fate, or fortune'. It therefore means 'one who influences fate or fortune'. It is a powerful word, much darker than fairy. Wilhelm Grimm also gave his sorceress a name—Mother Gothel—and a voice.

In earlier versions of the tale, there is little direct speech at all. Wilhelm Grimm, however, gives his characters voices, and none has so much to say as the sorceress. Rapunzel's mother speaks once, the father, the prince and Rapunzel each speak twice, but the sorceress speaks six times, including the haunting incantation, 'Rapunzel, Rapunzel, let down your hair', and her final unforgettable speech, in which she compares herself to a cat and tells the prince she shall scratch out his eyes (Bottigheimer 1987, p. 181). This is the last the sorceress is heard of or seen in the Grimm version. We never discover what happens to her after that.

The disappearance of the witch from the tale is an interesting omission, particularly since evil stepmothers are often given short shrift in Wilhelm's moral universe, punishments including dancing in red-hot shoes, being rolled down a hill in a barrel studded with nails, having mill-stones dropped on their heads, or being burnt to ashes. Such graphic and violent punishments reflect the historical practice of witch-hunts in Germany, with sorcery remaining punishable by law well into the late 18th century, when Wilhelm Grimm was a young boy.

Yet his sorceress is neither devoured, like Basile's ogress, nor moved to pity and mercy like La Force's fairy. She is simply never heard of again. Perhaps Wilhelm's recent loss of his own loving and somewhat suffocating mother was still too raw for him to punish a mother for being too over-protective. Perhaps his austere Calvinist soul was troubled by the story's themes of sexual desire and strange yearnings. Perhaps he simply could not bring himself to redeem the witch whose garden grows the parsley that causes the mother to pine away, the witch whose tower imprisons the growing young girl, the witch whose magic causes such unnatural burgeoning of her hair, the witch who can cause a young man to be so scarred and blinded.

The sorceress in the Grimm version is halfway between Basile's grotesque, anthropophagic ogress and the firm but loving fairy in La Force's tale. The Grimms' sorceress retains the sense of standing between wildness and civilisation, human and non-human, life and death. She is dangerous, but not hideous. She is cruel but not cannibalistic.

She is formidable, but not without vulnerabilities. The empowerment of the witch in the Grimms' version of the tale makes her a far more interesting character than she had been in Basile and La Force's earlier variants.

In *The Uses of Enchantment: The Meaning and Importance of Fairy Tales* (1975), Bruno Bettelheim takes note of the age at which Rapunzel was locked in the tower (the 1857 Grimm edition says that Rapunzel was twelve, a detail first added by La Force in 'Persinette'). Although Bettelheim's work has been criticised both for its heavy Freudian emphasis and its narrowness of focus (Zipes 1979, p. 181; Darnton 1985, p. 10), his work has been highly influential on later fairy tale scholarship.

Bettelheim writes: 'Hers is...the story of a pubertal girl, and of a jealous mother who tries to prevent her from gaining independence—a typical adolescent problem which finds a solution when Rapunzel becomes united with her prince' (p. 16). Bettelheim later notes that in a girl's oedipal fantasy, the mother is split into two figures: the pre-oedipal wonderful good mother and the oedipal evil stepmother (p. 114). This dichotomous view of the mother—true mother/false mother, kind mother/evil mother—has strong echoes of the Jungian archetypes of the 'Good Mother' who gives life and the 'Terrible Mother' who takes it away. The first is the bringer of life and fertility. The second is a devourer, a goddess of death and decay. As Joseph

Campbell wrote: 'She is the womb and the tomb: the sow that eats her farrow' (1993, p. 114).

Most critical interpretations of 'Rapunzel' focus on this symbiotic mother-daughter relationship. For example, Maria Tatar has written, 'Mother Gothel figures as the consummate overprotective parent' (2004, p. 55), and Sheldon Gould has stated: 'The witch's demand…serves to remind us that witches, despite their wicked nature, have maternal longings…Her decision to keep Rapunzel in the tower flowed not from malice but from maternal concern' (1999, pp. 157-160). Similarly, for Joan Gould, 'Rapunzel and her foster mother are White Bride and Black Mother. Rapunzel is first confined and then abandoned. The mother-witch's fury is what pushes the girl from one condition to the other' (2005, p. 217).

There are two problems with this interpretation of 'Rapunzel'. The first is that this split between the 'good mother' and the 'bad mother' is not actually an accurate representation of the roles of the female characters in this story. The 'true mother' gives in to her strange craving for forbidden food and so must pay the price by surrendering her daughter. The 'false mother' arguably locks her foster-daughter away because she intends to keep her safe from such dangerous desires. Nonetheless, both true and false mothers put their own fears and wants ahead of the well-being of the girl.

In addition, the false mother is the source of fecundity and life in the story, with her garden filled with lush greenery and her magic which causes Rapunzel's hair to grow to such luxuriant lengths that it can be used as a rope. The true mother is the one who is hungry, the one who devours the salad greens that give her daughter her name. She is the one who surrenders her daughter.

I thought about these matters a great deal in creating my character of the witch in *Bitter Greens*, for it is her voice and her story that makes up one of the three narrative threads. I needed to somehow make her a sympathetic character, despite all the evil that she does. Also, because I was writing a historical novel, I had to make sure that she was a woman with no greater supernatural powers than would have been believable in Renaissance Italy.

My research of the period had taught me that 16th century women of the Venetian Republic were kept tightly confined within certain roles. They were nuns, wives, or courtesans. Reading about the salons of the courtesans, where the discussion of art, music, literature and politics was as important as their sexual availability, I decided that my witch-figure—Selena Leonelli, called La Strega Bella or the beautiful witch—would be one of these *cortigiane onesta*. I read the biography of Veronica Franca, the most famous of the honest courtesans, and found a few horrifying facts about their lives that sparked ideas about what may have so misshapen a woman's life that she felt the need to lock another young woman away. Discovering there had been a deadly outbreak of bubonic plague in Venice in the 1580s, I wove that into her life also.

I had also discovered, during my research, that the 16th century Venetian artist Tiziano Vecelli (better known in English as Titian) had famously painted the same red-haired woman—believed to be a courtesan and his mistress—over and over again during the seventy-odd years of his artistic career. This was an extraordinary fit with what I had already planned for my witch, and so Selena became Titian's mysterious red-haired muse.

Finally, I needed to understand Renaissance Italian attitudes to witchcraft. My research led me to Carlo Ginzburg's *Night Battles: Witchcraft and Agrarian Cults in the Sixteenth and Seventeenth Century* (1966), which draws upon the official Inquisition archives from the 16th and 17th centuries. Ginzburg shows that the peasant culture of Renaissance Italy was deeply rooted in early European fertility cults which bear a striking similarity to Göttner-Abendroth's theory of an ancient matriarchal mythology. This belief system was called *La Vecchia Religione*, or the Old Religion. Female witches were called *strega* and male witches were called *stregone*, and their rituals were seasonal and ecstatic. Each village had a witch who was one of the 'Benandanti' (good walkers). On four ritual occasions of the year, they battled with the 'Malandanti' (evil walkers) in a conflict to protect the crops of the people. Confessions of these 'witches' were recorded by the Inquisition after 1575. I drew upon this research in my creation of the beliefs and practices of my witch Selena, as well as on the work of academics and anthropologists such as James Frazer and Marija Gimbutas.

Jungian psychologists believe the archetypal figure of the mother must be confronted and transcended in the process of individuation. In other words, a child must break free of the tie to the mother figure before he or she can grow into a strong and individual adult (Watts, Cockcroft & Duncan 2009, p. 246). This links back to Göttner-Abendroth's theories of the three-faced goddess: the role of the crone is always that of forcing transformation and change.

In terms of thinking through my representation in *Bitter Greens* of the relationship between Rapunzel and the witch, these readings helped me to conceive of the story as one surpassing that of a young-woman-as-prisoner. It is the story of a young woman, held in a state of stasis, who somehow finds the way to break free and be transformed from child to woman, from maiden to mother, from powerless prisoner to a powerful agent of birth, healing and redemption. None of this would be possible if she did not have to struggle against the figure of the dark feminine, the witch.

Indeed, in *Bitter Greens*, the reformed witch Selena in one sense gives birth to the maiden Margherita through her storytelling. She invents the girl, as she invents the tale, and so is the girl's metaphorical mother as much as midwife.

Although it is clear that Wilhelm Grimm's changes to the story diluted much of the agency of the heroine, his work also simplified and streamlined the story, and brought a freshness and poetic intensity to the language. When people think of 'Rapunzel', they think of the Grimms. It is their version—with the never-to-be-forgotten addition of the chant, 'Rapunzel, Rapunzel, let down your hair'—which entered popular imagination and did much to ensure the story's survival, as I explore further in the following chapter.

Chapter 6

Girls in Attics: The Descendants of Rapunzel

Since the Grimm brothers' version of 'Rapunzel' was first translated into English in the mid-19th century, there has been an astonishing array of retellings, reimaginings and revisionings of the tale, including poems, short stories, novels, operas, ballets, and animated children's films.

Feminist thinking about fairy tales in the 1970s would drive a lively reassessment about the gender politics of stories such as 'Rapunzel' and the power such tales have in shaping—and misshaping—women's 'psycho-sexual self-concepts' (Lieberman, quoted in Hasse 2004, p. 3). By the 1980s, feminist scholars proposed that 'myth, tale, and tragedy must be transformed by bold acts of reinterpretation in order to enter the experience of the emerging female self' (Heilbrun, quoted in Hasse 2004, p. 5).

Meanwhile, fairy tale studies by both men and women were rediscovering the female sources of many of the tales, from the long-ignored *conteuses* of the 17th century Parisian salons to the middle-class women who told the Grimm brothers so many of their most famous tales. Long-lost tales were revived, and long-known tales were illuminated by new understanding of their sources and evolution (Haase 2004, pp. 8-21).

Fairy tales studies nowadays are therefore deeply informed by new and sometimes ambivalent thinking about gender, politics, psychology, and society. This can create a kind of 'cognitive dissonance' (Haase 2004, p. 27) in readers of fairy tales and fairy tale retellings, who may on the one hand be entranced by the beauty of the tales and on the other hand feel guilty because of the tales' perceived role in upholding outmoded patriarchal and bourgeois views of society. As a writer working in the 21st century, it is impossible for me not to be aware of this dissonance, and also aware of the way retellers of tales must choose to maintain and reproduce the fairy tale framework, or to disrupt and transgress it (Preston, in Haase 2004, pp. 198-200).

It is also impossible for me to work without being acutely aware of the retellers of the tale who have gone before me, each reimagining the tale in new ways and so disrupting and destabilising the original sources. In this final section of my mythic biography of Rapunzel, I examine the most interesting and influential of these retellings and the ways in which they helped shape my own individual creative vision.

The Grimm brothers' *Kinder-und-Hausmärchen* was translated into English for the first time in 1823 by Edgar Taylor, but he saw Rapunzel as being too sexually provocative and so did not include it. This English translation, entitled *German Popular Stories,* was aimed specifically at children, and much of the violence, cruelty and sexuality was toned down, to make the stories, as David Blamires notes, 'more reassuring and less disturbing' (2009, p. 154). The book was beautifully illustrated by George Cruickshank, which was a major factor in its popularity.

Its unexpected success inspired Wilhelm and Jakob Grimm to produce their own children's edition, illustrated by their brother Ludwig, and generally called the 'Small Edition', published in late 1824. Wilhelm chose fifty-two stories, also excluding 'Rapunzel', although the story continued to be included in the *Kinder-und-Hausmärchen* 'Large Editions' until the final version published in 1857.

In 1846, 'Rapunzel' was translated into English for the first time by John Edward Taylor, cousin to Edgar Taylor, in a collection named *The Fairy Ring: A New Collection of Popular Tales*. The story was renamed 'Violet', and the pregnant mother craved the flowers of the violet to smell instead of green leaves to eat (Blamires 2009, pp. 160-161).

In 1853, a new translation of the Grimm tales appeared in a two-volume edition entitled *Household Stories*, published by Addey & Co. The books were illustrated by Edward H. Wehnert and it is believed he was also the translator, with the assistance of members of his German-speaking family (Blamires 2009, p. 163). In Wehnert's version, the plant is named as a radish and the girl is named Rapunzel, and so the symbolic link between the forbidden food and the girl is definitively broken.

Lucy Crane's collection was published in 1882 and illustrated by her brother Walter (Blamires 2009, p. 170). In this collection, the plant is named rampion and the girl Rapunzel (though the story states that these are the same). Lucy Crane's small collection was followed by the magisterial translation by Margaret Hunt in 1884, which included all scholarly notes.

The first creative response to the tale was made by the Victorian poet and artisan William Morris, who met the poet Edward Burne-Jones at Oxford in the 1850s. Both shared a love of all things medieval and magical, which led them to becoming friends with Dante Gabriel Rossetti, John Everatt Millais, and William Holman Hunt, founding members of the Pre-Raphaelite Brotherhood. It was probably Millais who introduced Morris to the Wehnert edition of the Grimm brothers' fairy tales, as he had been taught painting by Wehnert in Jersey as a boy (de la Sizeranne 2008, p. 161).

Morris's imagination was seized by the tales, and, in particular, the tale of 'Rapunzel'. He began work on a long poem with the same name in late 1857. It was around this time that Morris met his future wife, Jane Burden. In February 1858, he persuaded her to marry him. He was not quite twenty-five years old, and Jane was only eighteen. The same month, the publishers Bell & Daldy published *The Defence of Guenevere & Other Poems* at Morris's expense. 'Rapunzel' was the sixth of these poems, and has all the atmosphere of a dream, and the corresponding dreamlike disconnection from time and space. Although the poem was inspired by a story, there is no sense of narrative causality in the events.

The three key characters in Morris's 'Rapunzel' (the prince, the maiden and the witch) all speak in turn. The witch cries again and again, 'Rapunzel, Rapunzel, let down your hair!'; 'Rapunzel, Rapunzel, weep through your hair!'; 'Is there any who will dare, to climb up the yellow stair, glorious Rapunzel's golden hair?' (These lines seem to be the origin of the well-known catchphrase, 'Rapunzel, Rapunzel, let down your hair, so I may climb the golden stair.')

The poem is rich with sensuality. The prince, on seeing Rapunzel, cries:

Glowing all crimson in the fire
Of sunset, I behold a face,
Which sometime, if God give me grace,
May kiss me in this very place.

The next stanza begins: 'Evening in the tower', and Rapunzel speaks:

It grows half way between the dark and light;
Love, we have been six hours here alone,
I fear that she will come before the night,
And if she finds us thus we are undone.

The two then escape the tower: 'Now let us go, love, down the winding stair, with fingers intertwined'. Once the two are free, the prince reveals his name—Sebald—then renames Rapunzel:

Gold or gems she did not wear,
But her yellow rippled hair,
Like a veil, hid Guendolen!

Names, as Morris would well have known, are very important in fairy tales. The name Rapunzel was given to the maiden in the original Grimm source to remind her that her own mother had given her up in order to indulge her uncontrollable longing to eat the plant of that name. The name Guendolen, however, comes from the Welsh. The word *gwen* means 'white, fair, blessed' and *dolen* means 'ring, circle, or links in a chain'. The heroine's new name is filled with potent symbolism—a ring is an emblem of wholeness, completeness, and the circular pattern of life, death and rebirth, the cycle that has no beginning and no end. The prince—by giving the heroine a new name—has given her the chance for a new beginning.

After their crowning as king and queen, Prince Sebald says:

I took my armour off,
Put on king's robes of gold,
Over the kirtle green
The gold fell fold on fold.

This seems, to me, a clear decision, on the part of the prince, to put away his trappings of war, and to embrace principles of love and peace, symbolised by the 'green kirtle' of nature. The prince's choice exemplifies Morris's own passionate love of nature and the Pre-Raphaelites' philosophy of returning to an older, pre-industrial mode of life (Harvey & Press 1991, pp. 110-116).

Love clearly triumphs. Guendolen says, at the end of the poem:

I am so glad, for every day
He kisses me much the same way
As in the tower; under the sway
Of all my golden hair.

The witch, that inscrutable representation of the dark feminine in the poem, calls despairingly from hell:

Guendolen! Guendolen!
One lock of hair.

Recent feminist readings of Morris's work have highlighted his preoccupations with themes of love and redemption, and pointed to the extraordinary number of 'wise' and 'cunning women' in his work. Florence C. Boos, Professor of Victorian Literature at the University of Iowa, called his work 'explosively sexual' and said, 'the hero is always seeking, he is always guided by this inner ideal, which to him is associated with fertility, and with life, and with sexuality without guilt or malice or possessiveness' (2007).

With his poem 'Rapunzel', Morris looked below the surface of the Grimm fairy tale to find a story of an archetypal quest for self-realisation, a mythic journey of separation, initiation and return. He recognised the strong undercurrents of sexuality in the original fairy tale, understood its universal themes of love and longing and liberty, and gave voice to the powerful mythic archetypes of Maiden and Crone. His poem inspired both the sensual painting of *Rapunzel Sings From the Tower* by Frank Cadogan Cowper in 1908, and Lou Harrison's 1952 opera *Rapunzel*. For me, it is the sheer beauty, romance and sensuality of the poem which appeals and which I tried to capture in my own interpretation of 'Rapunzel'. I too wanted my work to be filled with symbolic images of life, love and redemption, and to hold within it a sense of the numinous, as well as of the sensuous. I used two quotations from the poem as epigraphs in *Bitter Greens* in homage to Morris, my favourite pre-Raphaelite.

Edith Nesbit is an author who certainly knew William Morris and his work, though 'Melisande', her light-hearted, comic *Rapunzel* retelling—published in 1901—is different in every way. Nesbit's family were friends of Dante Gabriel Rossetti and his sister Christina (the author of 'Goblin Fruit') and Edith herself friends with May Morris, William Morris's daughter.

Born in 1858, Nesbit met her future husband Hubert Bland at the age of eighteen and married him a few years later when she was seven months pregnant. The marriage was tempestuous and unconventional, with Nesbit raising her husband's two illegitimate children as well as her own three, and his mistress living with the family as their housekeeper and secretary. Refusing to wear the tight-fitting, figure-enhancing clothes of the era, Nesbit cut her hair short and rolled her own cigarettes (Campbell 2010, p. 64).

Being the primary breadwinner for the family after her husband was struck down with smallpox, Nesbit began to write with her first novel *The Story of the Treasure Seekers*, which was published in 1899. In her short story 'Melisande' (1901), the heroine is cursed by an evil fairy at her christening and grows up bald, but finds herself facing a whole other set of problems when her wish for golden hair is fulfilled:

'The Princess's hair began by being a yard long, and it grew an inch every night. If you know anything at all about the simplest sums you will see that in about five weeks her hair was about two yards long. This is a very inconvenient length. It trails on the floor and sweeps up all the dust, and though in palaces, of course, it is all gold-dust, still it is not nice to have it in your hair.' The king's fairy godmother suggested: 'Why not advertise for a competent Prince? Offer the usual reward.' (Nesbit, in Auerbach & Knoepflmacher 2014, p. 182)

The prince Florizel answered the advertisement, and was able to help break the curse, and the two married in the end. The story gently parodies the usual fairy tale style of the time and was applauded for 'mocking earlier stereotypes of females magnified by male desire' (Auerbach & Knoepflmacher, quoted in Campbell 2010, p. 64).

'Melisande' was thus the first reworking of 'Rapunzel' with a subversive (pre)feminist edge, something which I too wished to do in my own retelling. Similarly, Nesbit's story had a fresh and unusual mixture of realism and fantasy, which kept her work sharp and unsentimental and helped make it feel real, as if it had really happened. I also like to keep my fantasy strongly rooted in the real, and in *Bitter Greens* I wanted to create that feeling of aliveness and possibility. Nesbit has been called 'the first modern writer for children' by her biographer Julia Briggs (2000, p. xi). Earlier children's books were marked by their didacticism, but as attitudes towards the concept of childhood changed throughout the 19th century, so did the type of books being written for children. Nesbit was the first to set her tales of magical adventure in an ordinary, everyday setting that child readers would instantly recognise, and she was also one of the first to create child protagonists that were neither cloyingly perfect nor flat and one-dimensional. Her work signalled a cultural shift in children's literature towards works that challenged traditional models of thought and behaviour (Campbell 2010, p. 63), and she is acknowledged as being a strong influence on many later children's writers including Edward Eager, C.S. Lewis, and Nicholas Stuart Gray, the writer of the next significant Rapunzel retelling, over sixty years later.

Born in Scotland on 23 October 1922, Gray made up stories and plays from a young age to amuse his brothers and sisters, and to try and escape his unhappy childhood. Gray left home at the age of fifteen, finding work as an actor and stage manager. His first play was produced before he was twenty years old, and he turned to writing for children in 1949 after seeing a hundred or more children queuing up for the cinema and wondering why there was no comparable entertainment for them in the theatre. He wrote the play *Beauty and the Beast* as a result; it was shown at the Mercury Theatre in London in 1950. Gray wanted, he has said, 'to give the children a sense of magic. Nobody attends to this enough. They give them too much realism. They can see it all on the box, they can see frightful things there. But they're not being given a world to *escape* to...the world of the imagination. Children must have an escape line somewhere' (Wintle & Fisher 1974, p. 152).

The Stone Cage was published in 1963 and is a retelling of 'Rapunzel' from the point of view of the witch's cat. Gray's story line follows the basic plot of the well-known Grimm fairy tale, which had been translated into English in 1884 by Margaret Hunt. Her translation was based upon the 1857 edition of the Grimm's *Kinder-und-Hausmärchen*, in which the character of Rapunzel is at its most passive and childlike. There is no mention of any sex, or pregnancy, or birth of twins in that tale, and Rapunzel betrays herself to the witch by complaining how much heavier she is to pull up than the prince.

Within the narrow confines of that tale, Gray created a story that celebrates the redemptive power of love. Tomlyn the cat and Marshall the raven—natural enemies and rivals for the witch's rare expressions of affection—are united in their desire to save Rapunzel. They protect her from the witch, an old, ugly and malicious woman who craves power.

The story begins when the witch tricks a woodcutter into giving up his newborn daughter. He asks her what she intends to do with the baby.

'Mother Gothel answers the man's question in a small and faraway voice: "I will teach her my craft. Teach her to be the greatest and wickedest witch in all the world"' (p. 63). However, her plans are thwarted when Tomlyn and Marshall lay a spell on the little girl so that she is unable to work magic. Rapunzel grows to maturity, frustrating and angering the witch in her inability to remember even the simplest of spells.

The two conspirators bring a young man to the witch's garden in the hope he will rescue Rapunzel, but unwittingly, she betrays him by complaining how much heavier the witch is to pull up. He leaps from the tower and is blinded. Again, the cat and the raven work to bring Rapunzel and the prince together again, even though Rapunzel has been banished to the dark side of the moon. In the final confrontation, the raven tells the witch he no longer fears her. Rapunzel agrees, 'very clearly and gently: "I'm not afraid of Mother Gothel, either." The witch gave a shrill cry..."You must fear me! You must! Sorcery can only thrive on fear"' (p. 238).

Rapunzel's courage—and the bravery of her animal friends—together overcome the witch, who is transformed by the raven's magic into a bare and lifeless-looking tree. There she must stay, 'dead and dried, till a heart may grow inside' (p. 242). Rapunzel and her prince return to the human world, but the raven and the cat stay with the witch on the dark side of the moon, to look after her until she returns to being human. In the final scene, Tomlyn the cat pours a few drops of water on the tree's roots, and a small, green leaf uncurls from a bare twig. In this way, Gray shows how the animals' faithfulness and compassion to the witch, despite her wickedness, hold out the hope of her redemption.

As stated previously, *The Stone Cage* was the first spur to my desire to write my own retelling of 'Rapunzel'. Although I too wanted to show how courage and compassion can win out over malice, I always felt that Gray's heroine was too sweet and biddable, and that she must have suffered more in being confined within such a small space all of her life. I felt the story needed an extra charge of both dread and desire.

The next revisioning of 'Rapunzel' was to wrest the fairy tale back into the adult realm. It was the seventh poem in Anne Sexton's collection *Transformations (*1971), described by her as 'this book of odd tales / which transform the Brother Grimm' (p. 2).

Sexton was born Anne Gray Harvey in November 1928, into a comfortably middle-class family in Newton, Massachusetts. Her childhood was troubled. Her father was an alcoholic, her mother emotionally distant, and although she was close to her great-aunt, Anna Ladd Dingley, Sexton was later to accuse both Dingley and her father of incestuous abuse.

At the age of nineteen, Sexton eloped with Alfred Muller Sexton II (nicknamed Kayo). Her first daughter, Linda, was born in July 1953, and Sexton was diagnosed with post-natal depression. The birth of her second child, Joyce, in August 1955, triggered another wave of rage and despair. On her twenty-eighth birthday, she attempted suicide for the first time (Middlebrook 1991).

In 1957, Sexton began to write poetry, encouraged by her therapist Dr Martin Orne. She joined several Boston writing groups, meeting poets such as Maxine Kumin, Robert Lowell, and Sylvia Plath, who were to be highly influential to her writing. Her first book of poems, *To Bedlam and Part Way Back*, was published in 1960. Only five years later, Sexton received the Pulitzer Prize for Poetry for *Live or Die* (1966), the culmination of an extraordinary list of honours.

However, poetic inspiration began to fail her. Months followed in which she was unable to write. One day in 1970, she was talking on the telephone with Maxine Kumin about her writer's block, when Sexton mentioned the story of 'Snow White' which she felt reflected her own life. When Kumin said that she could not remember much about the tale, Sexton asked her daughter Linda to read the story to Kumin on the phone. As she listened 'little sparks' were fired in her imagination. Sexton began to see the possibility of writing a series of poems based upon fairy tales (Middlebrook 1991, p. 333).

The poem 'Rapunzel' (1971) begins:

A woman
who loves a woman
is forever young.

At once Sexton ruptures the usual reading of 'Rapunzel' as a story about an over-protective mother-figure, reframing it as a lesbian romance. This is a radical retelling of the traditional tale, subverting usual narrative expectations of the tale as a heterosexual love affair. The poem continues, a little further on:

Many a girl
had an old aunt
who locked her in the study
to keep the boys away.

Later, the 'old aunt'—the witch of the poem—implores the girl: 'Give me your nether lips / all puffy with their art / and I will give you angel fire in return'.

These erotic images may have been inspired by Sexton's relationship to her own 'old aunt', Anna Ladd Dingley, whom Sexton believed had molested her. The incident was told by Sexton to her psychotherapist Dr Orne in a 'trance-like state'. Certainly, there is no doubt that incest 'repeatedly surfaces, like a dark fin, in Sexton's work' (Hughes 1991). A recent analysis of her life and work by

Dawn Skorczewski concludes that Sexton was, in all probability, an incest survivor.

In this section of the poem, there are two references to water. The first, 'for I am at the mercy of rain' seems to reference both Rapunzel's healing tears and the sense of rain as a force of nature, pounding the narrator down. The second, 'the sea bangs into my cloister', extends the impression of strength and power and even violence of the lovers' meeting while also playing with the vernacular of the verb 'bang' as an euphemism for sexual intercourse. The sea, like all bodies of water, has always been associated with the feminine, as well as being a symbol of the subconscious, while a cloister (from the Latin *claustrum*, meaning enclosure) refers literally to a nunnery's inner garden and metaphorically to a woman's womb.

The poem is filled with images of gardens and plants: 'The yellow rose will turn to cinder', 'Let me hold your heart like a flower / lest it bloom and collapse', 'we lie together all in green / like pond weeds', 'They are as tender as bog moss'. The plant rampion is described as 'life-giving' twice, and at the end of the poem Rapunzel's tears are described as 'cure-alls', a reference to German rampion's common name 'king's cure-all'.

The poem finishes with the conclusion that 'mother-me-do / can be outgrown…just as a tricycle', intimating that the girl outgrew her love for the 'aunt' as she herself grew into womanhood.

The poem concludes 'only as she dreamed of the yellow hair, did moonlight sift into her mouth', a line of subtle beauty that is limned with the radiance of the moon, symbol of romantic love, while referencing ancient mythic beliefs of the moon as a goddess of powerful feminine magic.

Anne Sexton's poem *Rapunzel* was significant in the way it reframed the tale in a contemporary setting with contemporary language. It also disrupted expected readings of traditional fairy tales, opening them up to new ways of thinking. The poetry collection *Transformations* was thus one of the first works of creative narrative to subvert and even sabotage well-known fairy tales of the Western canon.

Sexton's work was inspired and informed by the immense social, political and philosophical upheaval of the 1960s, during which the norms of a patriarchal and bourgeois society were challenged and upset. New thinking about the role of women in society and about racial and sexual identity led to many new voices and forms of literary expression and a desire to give voice to those who had been rendered mute by society [9].

I have long been fascinated by Anne Sexton and her work, and first read *Transformations* in my undergraduate degree. I remember the shock and thrill of that first reading. I wanted to capture some of that electrifying charge of subversion and transformation in my novel *Bitter Greens*.

I also wanted to explore the possibility of a lesbian relationship between captor and captive, an interpretation of their relationship that seems impossible not to consider in light of new thinking about gender, sexuality and the body in the 21st century.

In the late 1990s, 'Rapunzel' was once again retold in novel form by Donna Jo Napoli, helping to spark a tsunami of fairy tale retellings for teenagers that is still rippling strongly today.

Donna Jo Napoli was born into a large Italian-American family in 1948. She never intended to become a writer, though she was an avid reader. After suffering a miscarriage, Napoli worked through her grief by writing letters to a friend, who saved them, telling her they should be turned into a novel. Napoli realised then that she loved to write, and she began to try her hand at stories (Crew 2010, p. 4).

One day her daughter, Eva, asked why there were so many mean women in fairy tales. Napoli's 'little feminist heart beat hard' in response (p. 19), and prompted her to write the award-winning *The Magic Circle*, a retelling of Hansel and Gretel told from the point of view of the witch.

Her next published novel was *Zel* (1996), a retelling of Rapunzel set in Switzerland in the mid-1500s. Napoli chose to tell the tale from three different points of view: Zel (a nickname for Rapunzel), her mother—who remains nameless—and Konrad (the son of a count). The story began from the point of view of Zel on the eve of her thirteenth birthday, a happy, curious child looking forward to the adventure of going to town. The narrative is written in the present tense, another unusual choice, perhaps used to heighten the sense of immediacy, perhaps to create a childish, living-in-the-moment voice.

The next chapter is a sharp change of gear, moving to the more formal, controlled first person voice of the mother. There is a cruel undertow to her voice. The cloth merchant angers her by saying her daughter must be nearly old enough to marry. The mother thinks: 'I would hiss at her…I could whisper to her of berries that turn poisonous as they roll into her mouth, of greens that catch in her throat and choke' (p. 18).

Meanwhile, back at the smithy, Zel meets a boy who is intrigued by her frankness and lack of deference. When Konrad gets home, it is to find his father has announced his betrothal to another girl. Konrad is horrified.

The next section is far darker and more psychologically intense. Once Mother realised Zel has met—and liked—a young man, she grows angry and tells Zel that she is taking her to 'a safe place', a tower abandoned many centuries before (p. 64). Zel lives alone in the tower for two years. Her mother visits her for only one hour every day. In the meantime, Konrad grows obsessed with finding Zel again. All experience a kind of madness: the mother unhinged by the possessiveness of her love, the daughter harrowed by her solitary imprisonment, a young man fixated on a girl he barely knows.

We discover the mother's motivations for her cruelty: she had been a barren woman who grew so fixated by her need to have her own child that she makes a Faustian deal with the Devil. Here, in the middle of the book—the psychic pivot of the story—Napoli retells the Rapunzel fairy tale in the mother's cold, precise, angry voice: 'One day the pregnant woman sent her beery husband on an errand of thievery. He climbed the wall and stole rapunzel. The barren woman watched him from the shadow of her home' (p. 132).

When the story returns to Zel's point of view, the narrative coherency has broken down, reflecting the emotional tumult of the imprisoned girl. Konrad finds her, watches Mother climb up, and then down, the braids of hair, and then climbs up them himself, before seducing Zel: 'He believes he might die, he might burst like the constellation of Perseus in August—a shower of shooting stars—but for her call, her cry…' (p. 180) It is a scene of intense and visceral sensuality, startling for its time.

The final scenes happen quickly, each shift between point of view quickening, each chapter only a few pages long. The plot line follows the traditional narrative trajectory. However, in Napoli's retelling, there was one clear distinction—the witch at once repents of her action and uses the very last of her strength to grow brambles around the tower to catch Konrad and save his life. The final words of the witch in the narrative were: 'He lives. I die.'

The final section is extremely brief, with the point of view changing to that of an omnipresent and omniscient narrator (where each previous chapter has named the narrator in the heading, this final the section is entitled simply 'All'). Blind and alone, Konrad wanders, drawn on by a force he cannot understand. Zel raises her daughters and creates with her hands, though 'fear can still seize her' (p. 214). The witch is still present in the narrative. She says: 'I watch the world. I have no powers anymore. I see as though through a goose eye.' Then, a few pages on, as Konrad gropes his way towards Zel, the witch says: 'I listen to the world. I have no powers anymore. I hear as though through a man's ears.' Zel weeps on Konrad's eyes and the final words of the book are: 'And they see each other and, yes, oh, yes, we are happy' (p. 227).

Zel is an extraordinary imaginative achievement, a dark, poetic, psychologically acute novel of obsessive love that gives the witch-figure a voice and a motivation for her actions, something that I hoped to do in *Bitter Greens*. I also loved Napoli's bravado in her willingness to play with language and allow the incoherency of her text to reflect the incoherency of a girl driven mad with her imprisonment. This too is something I like to do in my own writing, and a technique I employ in *Bitter Greens*.

Zel was to inspire a great many other young adult novels that draw upon fairy tales, including the 'Rapunzel' retellings *The Tower Room* by Adèle Geras, set in a 1960s girls boarding school (2005); *Golden: A Retelling of Rapunzel* by Cameron Dokey in which the heroine is born bald (2006); and *Letters from Rapunzel* by Sara Lewis Holmes which tells a the story of a modern-day girl whose father is battling with depression (2007). This new flowering of fairy-tale-inspired fiction for teenagers occurred at the same time as a general boom in the genre: between 1995 and 2005, there was a twenty-five per cent rise in the number of books published for young adults (Hill 2014, p. 3).

The number of 'Rapunzel'-inspired short stories also quickened, with eight such stories in the next eight years. The most striking are by Lisa Russ Spaar, Emma Donoghue, Tanith Lee and Beth Adele Long, whose story contains a section wittily entitled 'Instructions on How to Raise your Captor, Jailer, and Negative Mother Figure up Into a Tower by Your Hair.'

'Rapunzel' poems also continued to be written during this period, most notably by Gwen Strauss, Lisa Russ Spaar, and Nicole Cooley.[10] Strauss writes, in her poem 'The Prince': 'All my childhood I heard about love / but I thought only witches could grow it / in gardens behind walls too high to climb' (Beaumont & Carlson, p. 75).

In 'Rapunzel Shorn', Spaar writes: 'I'm redeemed, head light / as seed mote, as a fasting / girl's among these thorns, lips / and fingers bloody with fruit' (p. 74).

Cooley's poem 'Rampion' (p. 164) is concerned with the relationship between mothers and daughters: 'Once upon a time / a woman longed for a child, but see how one desire easily / replaces the next...'

Discovering these poems, and many others published in *The Poets' Grimm: 20th Century Poems from the Grimm Fairy Tales* (Beaumont & Carlson, 2003), was a delight; it led me to put extracts from my favourite 'Rapunzel' poems as epigraphs at the beginning of each section of *Bitter Greens*. I had a number of reasons for doing this. Firstly, I wanted to share these beautiful, powerful poems with others. Secondly, I wanted to use the poems to highlight the key themes or events in each separate section. For example, in one of the darkest sections of Charlotte-Rose's narrative, I use a poem by Arlene Ang in which the prince 'failed to see the woodpile / of chewed bones at the corner of the hearth.' Finally, I wanted to show that the

'Rapunzel' fairy tale continues to be as alive and relevant today as it was hundreds of years ago.

This relevance was amply demonstrated in 2008, when the husband-wife writing team, Shannon and Dean Hale, reinvented the tale as a wise-cracking, whip-cracking graphic novel set in the Wild West, illustrated with energy by Nathan Hale (no relation to the authors). Shannon was already a well-known reteller of fairy tales for a young adult audience; this collaboration was her husband Dale's first book.

Rapunzel's Revenge is an exuberant and funny version of the fairy tale, set in a mythic Wild West world. The heroine, Rapunzel, is the pampered yet lonely daughter of an immensely rich and powerful woman who has 'growth magic' which enables her to make plants grow far beyond their natural state. Rapunzel is troubled by dreams and curious about the world beyond her mother's hacienda, but is never permitted to see what lies beyond. On her twelfth birthday she manages to scale the high wall and sees that beyond the hacienda is a terrible industrial wasteland, devoid of trees, where countless people labour in mining pits among black-belching smoke-stacks. 'Well, I'll be swigger-jiggered and hung out to dry,' Rapunzel says (2008, p. 12).

The Rebirth of Rapunzel

Rapunzel climbs over the wall and goes down into the mining pits, where she at once meets her real mother and realises she had been snatched by Mother Gothel. The two are forcibly separated, and Rapunzel goes back to the hacienda to confront the woman she now knows is her kidnapper. Rapunzel is banished to an immensely tall tree in a swamp. In the tree, Rapunzel's hair grows 'ridiculously long'; she begins to use it as a skipping rope, as a whip to smack away spiders, and as a swing. One day she uses her hair to lasso another tree in the forest and rappels her way to freedom. Eventually she meets a rapscallion thief named Jack (who once climbed a beanstalk). They team up, and set out on a wild adventure to help the helpless and defeat Mother Gothel.

Rapunzel does most of the fighting, using her long, thin, red braids of hair like a lasso, while Jack is quick on his feet and quick with a joke. Together they grapple with outlaw gangs, surly henchmen, a pack of rabid coyotes and an ungrateful little girl, all the while avoiding their 'Wanted: Dead or Alive' posters. The story is told primarily through sharp and witty dialogue, allowing the illustrations to do most of the work.

When asked why she and her husband Dale chose the 'Rapunzel' fairy tale to parody, Hale answered: 'Rapunzel seemed to have built-in weapons of kick-butt proportions, besides suffering through one of the most pathetic fairy tales of all time in need of a serious makeover. (Why on earth didn't the prince just bring her a rope, for Pete's sake?)' (Blasingham 2010, p. 518). A good question, and one which I had to consider in my own very different retelling of the tale. For me, it was important that the heroine's escape from the tower was not too easy. She needed to struggle to find the strength and the courage and some kind of understanding of herself and the witch before she could break free.

Two years after the publication of *Rapunzel's Revenge*, Walt Disney Animation Studio released a funny, light-hearted retelling of the well-known Grimm tale entitled *Tangled*. It featured a girl who can use her magical hair as a lasso, and a wise-cracking thief as the hero. It is hard to believe the similarities between *Rapunzel's Revenge* and *Tangled* are mere coincidence. Shannon Hale certainly noticed the resemblances herself, tweeting in January 2011: 'Just watched *Tangled*. Feeling slightly violated.' (Hale 2011)

Released on 24 November 2010, *Tangled* was Walt Disney Animation Studio's fiftieth animated motion picture and their first to be shot in 3D. It cost the studio $260 million to create, making it the most expensive animated film ever to be made, but earned more than $590 million worldwide (Muljadi n.d., p. 366-387). The studio promoted it with the tagline: '*Tangled* is the ultimate story of breaking free after being grounded for life.'

The story, the studio announced in its publicity material, 'is based on the classic German fairy tale *Rapunzel* by the Brothers Grimm.' Most journalists added the adverb 'loosely'. That is probably an understatement. There is little remaining of the original story except for a girl in a tower, a witch, and a whole lot of hair.

Disney Animation Studios adroitly sidestepped most of the key moral dilemmas in the tale. Their heroine is not a poor girl sold for a handful of lettuce, but a beloved princess kidnapped from her bed. The tower is not a prison, but a vast and luxurious palace. Most importantly, it is not difficult for Rapunzel to leave her tower—she can simply abseil her way out anytime she pleases, thanks to the magical properties of her glowing, golden hair. The only bar to her freedom is her duty to the woman she thinks is her mother.

The film deliberately sets out to be light-hearted, fast-paced, and sentimental. It makes the occasional nod to its forebears, but always in as frivolous and amusing way as possible, as in the following dialogic exchange:

Flynn Rider: Alright, blondie…

Rapunzel: Rapunzel.

Flynn Rider: Gesundheit!

The narrative purpose of the movie is not to recount Rapunzel's escape from the tower—this occurs easily and joyously in a matter of seconds—

but rather her journey towards the unmasking of her false mother and finding her true parents.

Tangled has its moments of charm, despite its abandonment of many of the key motifemes of the plot, but the character of Mother Gothel is not one of them. She remains a cartoonish character, shallow and manipulative, with no moral ambiguity. As Mother Gothel says in *Tangled*, 'You want me to be the *bad* guy? Fine, now I'm the *bad* guy.'

One consequence of changing Rapunzel from a surrendered child to a stolen child is the alteration of the whole power mechanics of the tale. It is no longer what Bottigheimer calls 'a rise fairy tale', but rather becomes 'a restoration fairy tale'. The key difference, Bottigheimer explains in *Fairy Tales: A New History* (2009, pp. 11-13) is that in a restoration tale, the protagonist first loses, then—after a series of adventures and lessons—is returned to their proper social and economic status. However, in a 'rise fairy tale', the story begins with 'a dirt-poor girl or boy who suffers the effects of grinding poverty and whose story continues with tests, tasks, and trials until magic brings about a marriage to royalty and a happy accession to great wealth' (2009, p. 11-12). The former upholds the socio-political status quo. The latter holds out the hope for social-political change.

Zipes said in an 2013 interview that 'the Disney promoters should have called the film *Mangled* because of the way it slaughtered and emptied the meaning of the Grimms' and other 'Rapunzel' folk tales... The major conflict is between a pouting adolescent princess and a witch. The Disney films repeatedly tend to demonize older women and infantilize young women. Gone are any hints that 'Rapunzel' might reflect a deeper initiation ritual in which wise old women keep young girls in isolation to protect them' (Cotfield & Hirai 2013, p. 3).

Disney's abandonment of the key motifemes of the 'Rapunzel' tale and its messages about growth, transformation, and the hard journey towards wisdom shows that there is no steady 'evolution' from conservative attitudes to less conservative ones with the passing of time. Each teller makes their own individual choices in what aspects of the tale are to be preserved or abandoned, and thus even a story as full of camouflaged mythic power as 'Rapunzel' has the potential to be drained of all meaning whatsoever.

The Disney film *Tangled* did not have any creative influence on me, simply because I did not watch it until after I had written the first few drafts of my novel. However, I have included the animated fantasy here because it is impossible to examine any fairy tale without looking at its interpretation by the Disney studios, the most influential and in many ways controversial purveyor of fairy tales in contemporary times. Besides, it seems somehow fitting to bookend my mythic biography of Rapunzel between the great psychodrama of life, death and rebirth told in the oral tales of an ancient gynocentic religion and the frivolous, female-reductive whimsy that is *Tangled*. As Marina Warner writes: 'this process of loss has to be resisted' (1994, p. 417).

Right from the beginning of my creative journey, I wanted to restore the mythic power I sensed in 'Rapunzel'. The more I read, the more urgent this desire became for me.

As explored earlier, I feel 'Rapunzel' continues to be told and retold because it is a tale about escape. However, as this exegesis has outlined, it also has a deeper mythic resonance. The quintessential symbols and structural patterns of 'Rapunzel' are those of ancient tales that celebrate the ritual wounding and death of both heroine and hero in their journey through darkness and fear towards brightness and courage. I feel that we discard such metaphorical meaning at our own peril, and that it is my job—as a storyteller, poet and novelist—to strive to keep such wisdom alive.

Conclusion
The Rebirth of Rapunzel

I began by wanting to retell a tale that has haunted my imagination since I was a child.

My desire led me on a journey that was far more difficult than I could ever have imagined. I had to discover the lost life of Charlotte-Rose de Caumont de La Force, the woman who wrote the tale as it is best known. I had to write three separate narrative threads, each set in a different time and place, each requiring an immense amount of research to bring the world of the story to life. I had to imagine myself into the skin of a woman who locked girls away from the world, and I had to imagine what it would be like to be one of those girls. I read and pondered hundreds of books, articles, stories and poems, and I wrote hundreds of thousands of words.

It took me seven years, a potent fairy tale number. Seven years spent wandering through the thorn-tangled forests of fairy tale, often afraid that I was lost, even more often afraid that I would fail. I struggled for a long time with the technical difficulties of writing such a complex novel, with my worry that it was all taking so long and was so hard and I was keeping my publishers waiting, with my anxiety that I was not a good enough writer to pull off all I was trying to do.

In this exegesis, I have articulated my motivations and purposes in re-telling 'Rapunzel', an ancient tale of terror and transformation, desire and deceit, imprisonment and escape, romance and redemption.

At first, I wished to understand why it is that this fairy tale has had such a fierce hold on my own imagination. I wanted to re-create some of the beauty and mystery and romance of the tale, which first enchanted me as a child; and I hoped to explore some of the more troubling aspects of the tale, the darkness and cruelty and eroticism ignored by those retellings of the tale which depicted a smiling maiden combing her hair in a rose-decorated turret. I also wished to rescue Rapunzel from the widely held misconception that she was 'a passive princess waiting patiently for her prince to come' (Wolf 2008, p. 167).

As I studied the tale in depth, my motivations became more complex. My discovery of La Force's life and work spoke strongly to my own feminism. Why is Charles Perrault remembered, I wondered angrily, when the women writers of the same era are forgotten? What about Marie-Catherine Le Jumel de Barneville, the Baroness d'Aulnoy, who invented the term 'fairy tale' and who was published before Perrault? What about Catherine Bernard, author of 'Riquet with the Tuft', Marie-Jeanne L'Héritier de Villandon, Perrault's niece and collaborator, or Henriette-Julie de Castelnau, the Countess of Murat and La Force's cousin? Their stories are extraordinary, beautiful and powerful, and yet they are scarcely known outside academia. I felt an urgent need to rescue them also, to celebrate their lives and works, and to waken the rest of the world to their stories.

My discovery of La Force and her circle of brilliant, clever and largely forgotten female *conteuses* also connected very strongly to a deep and abiding preoccupation of mine: the necessity of storytelling. Implicit in the broad-ranging and sometimes strident arguments about fairy tales and gender is the belief that the stories of our society help shape who we are. Most famously, the 1970s feminist Marcia R. Lieberman has written: 'millions of women must surely have formed their psycho-sexual self-concepts, and their ideas of what they could or could not accomplish, what sort of behaviour would be rewarded and of the nature of the reward itself, in part from their favourite fairy tales' (in Haase 2004, p. 3). Equally implicit, then, must be the idea that one way to change the shape of who we are is to change the stories we tell.

This concept is at the heart of a movement in feminist creative arts that Jane Caputi called 'psychic activism'. She appeals to female creative artists to actively bring about—by a reworking of the world's symbols, myths and language—an evolutionary shift in consciousness. 'One of the most significant developments to emerge out of the contemporary feminist movement was the quest to reclaim that symbolising / naming power, to refigure the female self from a gynocentric perspective, to discover, revitalise and create a female oral and visual mythic tradition and use it, ultimately, to change the world', Caputi wrote (Larrigton 1992, p. 425).

Monica Sjöö and Barbara Mor express the same aims in other words: 'Witches cast spells, not to do evil but to promote changes of consciousness. Witches cast spells as acts of redefinition. To respell the world means to redefine the root of our being. It means to redefine us and therefore change us' (1987, p. 425). If we can change the tale, we can change the world.

What I have come to realise is that some kind of psychic activism is at the heart of what I try to do in my storytelling. I am hoping to use old myths and tales in order to create new ones. I am retelling this old tale, in order to respell the world.

For me, 'Rapunzel' is such an old, wise story, yet its archetypal wisdom is veiled by centuries of dust and cobwebs. In my novel *Bitter Greens* and in this exegesis, I'm trying to blow off those cobwebs and rub away the tarnish, hoping to make the brightness of the original myth shine out once more.

The journey has not been easy for me. Writing about my childhood illnesses has stirred up many unhappy memories that I had thought laid to rest long ago. Some scenes in *Bitter Greens* were so dark and disturbing they were difficult to write, and I suffered nightmares and anxiety as a result. The writing itself took so long and was at times so exhausting it took its toll on my loved ones as well on me: 'Why couldn't you just write a simple fairy tale retelling like everyone else!' my husband exclaimed at one point.

Yet one thing that studying 'Rapunzel' has taught me is that all growth comes at some cost. To gain some kind of profound transformation, we need to undertake that journey into darkness, that symbolic wounding and death, before we can again travel upwards into light and understanding. Rapunzel had to have her long braid of hair cut off and be cast out of the tower to wander alone in the wilderness, before she could become the mother and queen and goddess she was meant to be.

So, in choosing to retell this tale, I was like a sorceress or a hag, the crone whose symbolic function is to be 'a midwife to the psyche' (Caputi, in Larrington 1992, p. 433). I stood on the threshold between the story's past and the story's possible future, one foot in green shadows, one foot in blazing light, one hand drawing out a thread, one hand wielding the snip-snap of shears. I was the midwife at Rapunzel's rebirth, and my own.

Endnotes

1 A meme is a unit of cultural information such as a story, a song, or a superstition, which replicates itself across cultures or over generations in a similar fashion to a gene. The word was coined by Richard Dawkins in his 1976 book *The Selfish Gene*, and popularised in fairy tales studies by Jack Zipes (2006, 2012). A memeplex is, according to psychologist Susan Blackmore, a group of memes that are replicated together (1996, p. 19). I explore the concept more fully in Chapter 1.

2 In my study of 'Rapunzel', I have drawn upon the structural theories of folklorist Alan Dundes, in which he foregrounds the importance of examining any folk tale though a comparison of motifemes (an abstract unit of action within a tale), motifs (the manifestation of a motifeme in an individual tale) and allomotifs (the manifestation of a motifemes in an array of similar tales) (Hasse 2008, p. 645).

3 My translator Sylvie Poupard-Gould worked from the original 17th century text *Les Fées Contes des Contes, par Mademoiselle de X*, published in 1967 and printed as a photocopy by Lightning Source UK Ltd, on my request, in 2010.

4 The letters of Elisabeth Charlotte, the Duchesse d'Orléans (trans. Forster, 1984) were most useful to me, though I also read the letters of Madame de Sevigné (edited by Mrs Hale in 1869) and the memoir and letters of Ninon de Lenclos (collected and translated by A Lady in 1761).

5 My primary sources were biographies and non-fiction books about the reign of Louis XIV by Antonia Fraser, Lisa Hilton, W.H. Lewis, and Anne Somerset. Please see bibliography for more details.

6 Please refer to the Appendix and Bibliography.

7 In some variants of the tale, Zal refuses to climb up the hair ladder as he does not wish to hurt Rudâbeh and so he throws up a rope to her instead (Fee 2011, p. 194).

8 I have drawn upon Jack Zipes' translation of 'Persinette', published in *The Great Fairy Tale Tradition* (2001, pp. 479-484).

9 Anne Sexton's work helped ignite an explosion of feminist fairy tale scholarship in the work of such scholars as Sandra Gilbert, Susan Gubar, Marcia R. Lieberman and Mary Daly, which then reverberated in the stories and novels of such writers as Robin McKinley, Angela Carter, Margaret Atwood, Tanith Lee and Terri Windling, who all wrote strikingly original and often revolutionary fairy tale retellings in the decades to follow. Much as I would love to discuss their work, the length restrictions of this exegesis mean that I, unfortunately, cannot.

10 These poems all appeared in Beaumont & Carlson 2003. Please see the Appendix for a list of other 'Rapunzel'-inspired novels, short stories and poems.

11 I compiled this list of 'Rapunzel' retellings with the help of Heidi Anne Heiner's Sur La Lune Fairy Tale website and Terri Windling's article on Rapunzel at the Journal of Mythic Arts. I am sure there are many other 'Rapunzel' retellings that I have missed, or which were created after I had finished my exegesis. I hope to discover them in time.

Appendix

Retellings of 'Rapunzel'

Adult Novels

Forsyth, K. 2012, *Bitter Greens,* Random House Australia.

Children's & Young Adult Novels

Durst, S. 2007, *Into the Wild,* Razorbill, USA.

Durst, S. 2008, *Out of the Wild,* Razorbill USA.

Flinn, A. 2013, *Towering,* HarperTeen, USA.

Dokey, C. 2006, *Golden: A Retelling of 'Rapunzel',* Simon Pulse, USA.

Geras, A. 1990, *The Tower Room,* Hamish Hamilton, UK.

Gray, N.S. 1963, *The Stone Cage*, Dennis Dobson, UK.

Hilton, K.C. 2013, *My Name is Rapunzel,* Amazon Digital Services, USA.

Mason, J.B. & Stephens, S.H. 2004, *Princess School: Let Down Your Hair,* Scholastic, USA.

Masson, S. 2014, *The Crystal Heart,* Random House, Australia.

Meyer, M. 2014, *Cress,* Feiwel & Friends, USA.

Mlynowski, S. 2014, *Whatever After #5: Bad Hair Day*, Scholastic Press, USA.

Napoli, D.J. 1996, *Zel*, Puffin Books, USA.

Robins, M.E. 2013, *Sold for Endless Rue,* Forge, USA.

Turgeon, C. 2013, *The Fairest of Them All,* Touchstone, USA.

Picture Books & Graphic Novels

Berenzy, A. 1996, *Rapunzel,* Henry Holt, USA.

Gibbs, S. 2011, *Rapunzel*, Harper Collins Children's Books, USA.

Hale, D. & Hale, S. 2008, *Rapunzel's Revenge*, Bloomsbury Children's Books, USA.

Holmes, S. 2007, *Letters from Rapunzel*, Harper Collins, USA.

Impey, R. & Bailey, P. (illust.) 2001, *Rapunzel and Rumpelstiltskin*, Orchard Books, USA.

Lisi, V. 1995, *Rapunzel,* Leopard Books, UK.

Matthews, C. & Blackwood, F. (illust.) 2005, *Emily's Rapunzel Hair*, ABC Books, Australia.

Rogasky, B. & Hyman, T.S. (illust.) 1982, *Rapunzel,* Holiday House, USA.

Stanley, D. 1997, *Petrosinella. A Neapolitan Rapunzel,* Puffin Reprint, USA.

Storace, P. & Colón, R. (illust.) 2007, *Sugar Cane: A Caribbean Rapunzel*, Jump at the Sun, USA.

Wilcox, L. & Monks, L. (illust.) 2003, *Falling for Rapunzel*, Putnam Juvenile, USA.

Zelinsky, P.O. 1995, *Rapunzel,* Dutton, USA.

Appendix & Bibliography

Short Stories & Novellas

Basile, G. [1634] 2001, 'Petrosinella' in Zipes, J. (ed.), *The Great Fairy Tale Tradition,* W.W. Norton & Co, USA, pp. 475-478.

Berliner, J. 2004, 'After the Flowering' in Greenberg, M. H. & Helfers, J. (eds.), *Little Red Riding Hood in the Big Bad City*, DAW, USA, n.p.

Bishop, A. 1997, 'Rapunzel' in Datlow, E. & Windling, T. (eds.), *Black Swan, White Raven*, Avon Books, USA, pp.122-141.

Bradley, J. 2013, *Beauty's Sister*, Penguin Books, Australia.

Crane, L. [1886] 1973, *Grimm's Fairy Tales,* Crown Publishers, USA, pp. 32-36.

Donoghue, E. 1997, 'The Tale of the Hair' in *Kissing the Witch*, HarperCollins, USA, pp. 83-99.

Friesner, E. 2000, 'Big Hair' in Datlow, E. & Windling, T. (eds.), *Black Heart, Ivory Bones*, Avon Books, USA, pp. 23-37.

Frost, G. 1995, 'The Root of the Matter' in Datlow, E. & Windling, T. (eds.), *Snow White, Blood Red*, Avon Books, USA, pp. 161-195.

Goldsworthy, K. 1984, 'Rapunzel, Rapunzel' in *Meanjin*, Summer issue, Vol. 43 no. 4, Australia, pp. 563-572.

Gonzenbach, L. (collector) [1870] 2004, 'Beautiful Angiola' in Zipes, J. (ed., trans.), *Beautiful Angiola: The Great Treasury of Sicilian Folk and Fairy Tales,* Routledge, USA, pp. 47-51.

Grimm, J. & W. [1857] 2001, 'Rapunzel' in Zipes, J. (ed.) *The Great Fairy Tale Tradition*, W.W. Norton & Company, USA, pp. 489-491.

Klein, D. 2009, 'The Girl in the Tower' in *There was once... The Collected Fairy Tales*, Moth Woman Press, Australia, pp. 6-7.

La Force, C-R. [1697] 1999 'Parslinette' in Zipes, J. (ed.), *Spells of Enchantment*, Penguin Books, USA, pp. 115-121.

La Force, C-R. [1697] 2001, 'Persinette' in Zipes, J. (ed.), *The Great Fairy Tale Tradition,* W.W. Norton & Company, USA, pp. 479-483.

La Force, C-R. [1697] 2010, Poupard-Gould, S. (trans. for the author), *Les Contes des Contes, par Mademoiselle de X*, Lightning Source UK Ltd.

Lee, T. 1983, 'The Golden Rope' in *Red as Blood or Tales From the Sisters Grimmer,* DAW, USA, pp. 66-95.

Lanagan, M. 2011, 'The Golden Shroud' in *Yellowcake*, Allen & Unwin, Australia, pp. 35-48.

Lee, T. 2000, 'Rapunzel' in Datlow, E. & Windling, T. (eds.), *Black Heart, Ivory Bones,* Avon Books, USA, pp. 4-19.

Long, B. A. 2005, 'Rapunzel Dreams of Knives' in *Strange Horizons* (October 17, 2005 issue), USA.

Lynn, E. 1995, 'The Princess in the Tower' in Datlow, E. & Windling, T. (eds.), *Snow White, Blood Red*, Avon Books, USA, pp. 196-213.

Marillier, J. 2005, 'Let Down Your Hair' in *Prickle Moon*, Ticonderoga Publications, Australia, pp. 47-52.

Metzger, L. 2003, 'The Girl in the Attic' in Datlow, E. & Windling, T. (eds.), *Swan Sister: Fairy Tales Retold*, Simon & Schuster, 2003, USA, pp. 82-92.

McKinley, R. 1994, 'Touk's House' in *A Knot in the Grain and Other Stories*, Greenwillow, UK, pp. 75-105.

Nesbit, E. 1901, 'Melisande' in *Nine Unlikely Tales*, Fisher Unwin, USA, n.p.

Nix, G. 2009, 'An Unwelcome Guest' in Datlow, E. & Windling, T. (eds.), *Troll's Eye View*, Viking Juvenile, USA, pp. 29-46.

Parks, R. 1999, 'Thy Golden Stair' in Little, D. (ed.) *Twice upon a Time,* DAW, USA, pp. 139-156.

Scheckley, R. 2004, 'Rapunzel: The True Story', in Little, D. (ed.), *Rotten Relations*, DAW, USA, n.p.

Slatter, A. 2010, 'Little Radish' in *Sourdough & Other Stories*, Tartarus Press, UK, pp. 33-44.

Spaar, L. 1997, 'Rapunzel's Exile' in Datlow, E. & Windling, T., *The Year's Best Fantasy and Horror: Tenth Annual Collection*, St. Martin's Press, USA, pp. 315-316.

Stegner, W.E. 1956, 'Maiden in a Tower' in *The City of the Living, and Other Stories,* Houghton Mifflin, USA, n.p.

Wade, S. 1995, 'Like a Red, Red Rose' in Datlow, E .& Windling, T. (eds.), *Snow White, Blood Red*, Avon Books, USA, pp. 21-49.

Poetry

Ang, A. 2007, 'Rapunzel', quoted in Windling, T. 2007, 'Rapunzel, Rapunzel, Let Down Your Hair', Mythic Passages of Imagination, Website, Accessed 6 August 2014, http://www.mythicjourneys.org/ newsletter_jul07_windling.html

Bennett, B. 2003, 'The Skeptical Prince' in *The Poets' Grimm: 20th Century Poems from Grimm Fairy Tales,* Beaumont J.M. & Carlson, C. (eds.), Story Line, USA, p. 124.

Broumas, O. 2003, 'Rapunzel' in *The Poets' Grimm: 20th Century Poems from Grimm Fairy Tales,* Beaumont J.M. & Carlson, C. (eds.), Story Line, USA, p. 141.

Cooley, N. 2003 'Rampion', *The Poets' Grimm: 20th Century Poems from Grimm Fairy Tales,* Beaumont J.M. & Carlson, C. (eds.), Story Line, USA, p. 164.

Crapsey, A. 1915, 'Rapunzel' in *Verse,* The Manas Press, USA, n.p.

Dolin, S. 2003, 'Jealousy' in Beaumont J.M. & Carlson, C. (eds.),*The Poets' Grimm: 20th Century Poems from Grimm Fairy Tales,* Story Line, USA, p. 99.

Friman, A. 2003, 'Rapunzel' in Beaumont J.M. & Carlson, C. (eds.), *The Poets' Grimm: 20th Century Poems from Grimm Fairy Tales*, Story Line, USA, p. 123.

Hay, S.H. 1998, 'Rapunzel' in *Story Hour*, University of Arkansas Press, USA, n.p.

Hemphill, E. 2003, 'Song for Rapunzel' in Beaumont J.M. & Carlson, C. (eds.), *The Poets' Grimm: 20th Century Poems from Grimm Fairy Tales*, Story Line, USA, p. 143.

Hewett, D. 2003, 'Grave Fairytale' in Beaumont J.M. & Carlson, C. (eds.), *The Poets' Grimm: 20th Century Poems from Grimm Fairy Tales*, Story Line, USA, p. 191.

Hillman, B. 2003, 'Rapunzel' in Beaumont J.M. & Carlson, C. (eds.), *The Poets' Grimm: 20th Century Poems from Grimm Fairy Tales*, Story Line, USA, p. 134.

Morris, W. 1858, 'Rapunzel' in *The Defence of Guenevere and Other Poems*, Ellis & White, UK, p. 111-134.

Sajé, N. 'Rampion' in Beaumont J.M. & Carlson, C. (eds.), *The Poets' Grimm: 20th Century Poems from Grimm Fairy Tales*, Story Line, USA, p. 111.

Schulz, F. [1790] 2001, 'Rapunzel' in Zipes, J. (ed.), *The Great Fairy Tale Tradition*, W.W. Norton & Company, USA, pp. 484-488.

Sexton, A. [1971] 1999, 'Rapunzel' in *Transformations*, Houghton Mifflin Co, USA, n.p.

Spaar, L.R. 2003, 'Rapunzel Shorn' in Beaumont J.M. & Carlson, C. (eds.), *The Poets' Grimm: 20th Century Poems from Grimm Fairy Tales*, Story Line, USA, p. 74.

Spaar, L.R. 2003 'Rapunzel's Clock' in Beaumont J.M. & Carlson, C. (eds.), *The Poets' Grimm: 20th Century Poems from Grimm Fairy Tales*, Story Line, USA, p. 112.

Strauss, G. 2003, 'The Prince' in Beaumont J.M. & Carlson, C. (eds.), *The Poets' Grimm: 20th Century Poems from Grimm Fairy Tales*, Story Line, USA, p. 75.

Terrone, M. 2003, 'Rapunzel: A Modern Tale' in Beaumont J.M. & Carlson, C. (eds.), *The Poets' Grimm: 20th Century Poems from Grimm Fairy Tales*, Story Line USA, p. 193.

Trinidad, D. 2003, 'Rapunzel' in Beaumont J.M. & Carlson, C. (eds.), *The Poets' Grimm: 20th Century Poems from Grimm Fairy Tales*, Story Line, USA, p. 73.

Untermeyer, L. 1920, 'Rapunzel' in *The New Adam*,
Harcourt, Brace & Howe, USA, n.p.

Yolen, J. 1989, 'The Golden Stair' in *The Faery Flag: Stories and Poems of Fantasy and the Supernatural*, Orchard, USA, n.p.

Bibliography

Albertson, E. & Albertson, M. 2002, *Temptations: Igniting the Pleasure and Power of Aphrodisiacs,* Fireside, USA.

Andresen, J.J. 1980, *'Rapunzel: The Symbolism of the Cutting of Hair'* in Journal of the American Psychoanalytical Association, pp. 69-88.

Ang, A. 2007, 'Rapunzel', quoted in Windling, T. 2007, 'Rapunzel, Rapunzel, Let Down Your Hair', Mythic Passages of Imagination, Website, Accessed 6 August 2014, http://www.mythicjourneys.org/ newsletter_jul07_windling.html

Auerbach, N. & Knoepflmacher U.C. 2014, *Forbidden Journeys: Fairy Tales & Fantasies by Victorian Women,* University of Chicago Press, USA.

Bacchilega, C. 1993, 'An Introduction to the "Innocent Persecuted Heroine" Fairy Tale', *Western Folklore,* Vol. 52, No. 1, Jan. 1993, Western States Folklore Society, USA, pp. 1-12.

Barbier, P. 1996, *The World of the Castrati: The History of an Extraordinary Operatic Phenomenon*, Souvenir Press Ltd, UK.

Basile, G. [1634] 2001, 'Petrosinella' in Zipes, J. (ed.), *The Great Fairy Tale Tradition*, W.W. Norton & Company, USA, pp. 475-478.

Beaumont, J.M. & Carlson, C. (eds.), 2003, *The Poets' Grimm: 20th Century Poems from the Grimm Fairy Tales*, Story Line, USA.

Bettelheim, B. 1976, *The Uses of Enchantment: The Meaning & Importance of Fairy Tales*, Vintage Books, UK.

Biddle-Perry, G. & Cheang, S. 2008, *Hair: Styling, Culture & Fashion*, Berg, UK.

Blackmore, S. 1999, *The Meme Machine*, Oxford University Press, UK.

Blamires, D. 2009, *Telling Tales: The Impact of Germany on English Children's Books 1780-1918*, Open Book Publishers, UK.

Blasingame, J. 2010, 'Interview With Shannon Hale About Rapunzel's Revenge', *Journal of Adolescent & Adult Literacy*, March 2010, Vol. 53 Issue 6, Wiley-Blackwell, USA, p. 518.

Boos, F.C. 2007, 'Medea and Circe as "Wise Women" in the Poetry of William Morris and Augusta Webster' in Latham, D. (ed.), *Writing on the Image: Reading William Morris*, University of Toronto Press, Canada, pp. 43-60.

Bottigheimer, R.B. 1987, *Grimms' Bad Girls & Bold Boys: The Moral and Social Vision of the*

Tales, Yale University Press, USA.

Bottigheimer, R.B. 2009, *Fairy Tales: A New History*, Excelsior Editions, State University of New York Press, USA.

Bottigheimer, R.B. 2012, *Fairy Tales Framed: Early Forewords, Afterwords and Critical Words*, SUNY Press, USA.

Briggs, J. 2000, *A Woman of Passion: The Life of E. Nesbit*, New Amsterdam Press, UK.

Briggs, R. 1996, *Witches & Neighbours: The Social and Cultural Context of European Witchcraft*, Blackwell Publishers, UK.

Brooke, C. 2001, *The Age of the Cloister: The Story of Monastic Life in the Middle Ages*, Hidden Spring, USA.

Brown, P.F. 1997, *Art and Life in Renaissance Venice*, Prentice Hall, USA.

Bryer, R. 2000, *The History of Hair: Fashion & Fantasy Down the Ages*, Philip Wilson, USA.

Cadogan, F.C. 1908, *Rapunzel Sings From the Tower,* pencil & watercolour with gum arabic, heightened with touches of bodycolour, 67.3 x 42 cm, The De Morgan Centre, London.

Carter, A. 2003, 'Introduction', *The Virago Books of Fairy Tales,* Virago, UK.

Crane, L. [1886] 1973, *Grimm's Fairy Tales,* Crown Publishers, USA.

Campbell, J. [1949] 1993, *The Hero With A Thousand Faces,* Fontana Press, USA.

Campbell, L.M. 2010, *Portals of Power—Magical Agency & Transformations in Literary Fantasy*, McFarland & Co., USA.

Canepa, N.L. 1999, *From Court to Forest: Giambattista Basile's* Lo Cunto De Li Cunti *and the Birth of the Literary Fairy Tale*, Wayne State University Press, USA.

Canepa, N. 2012, 'Giambattista Basile: 1575?-1632' in Raynard, S. (ed.), *The Teller'sTale: Lives of the Classic Fairy Tale Writers*, State University of New York Press, pp. 25-27.

Caputi, J. 1992, 'On Psychic Activism: Feminist Mythmaking' in Larrington, C. (ed.), *The Feminist Companion to Mythology*, Pandora Press, UK, pp. 425-440.

Caputi, J. 1993, *Gossips, Gorgons & Crones: The Fate of the Earth*, Inner Traditions, USA.

Caputi, J. 2004, *Goddesses & Monsters: Women, Myth, Power & Popular Culture*, Popular Press, USA.

Cashdan, S. 1999, *The Witch Must Die: The Hidden Meaning of Fairy Tales*, Basic Books, USA.

Chamberlin, E. R. 1982, *The World of the Italian Renaissance*, George Allen & Unwin, UK.

Cohen, E. & Cohen T. 2001, *Daily Life in Renaissance Italy*, The Greenwood Press, USA.

Cooley, N. 2003, 'Rampion', *The Poets' Grimm: 20th Century Poems from Grimm Fairy Tales*, Beaumont J.M. & Carlson, C. (eds.), Story Line, USA, p. 164.

Cooper, W. 1971, *Hair: Sex, Society, Symbolism*, Stein & Day, USA.

Crew, H.S. 2010, *Donna Jo Napoli—Writing with Passion*, Scarecrow Press, USA.

Daly, M. [1978] 1990, *Gyn/Ecology: The Metaethics of Radical Feminism*, Beacon Press, USA.

Darnton, R. 1985, *The Great Cat Massacre and Other Episodes in French Cultural History*, Vintage Books, USA.

Daniel, E.L & Mahdi, A.A. 2006, *Culture and Customs of Iran*, Greenwood Press, USA.

Datlow, E. & Windling, T. (eds.), 1993, *Snow White, Blood Red*, Signet, USA.

Davis, R.C. & Ravid B. (eds.), 2001, *The Jews of Early Modern Venice,* Johns Hopkins University Press, USA.

De la Sizeranne, R. 2008, *The Pre-Raphaelites,* Parkstone Press International, USA.

De Lenclos, N. [1620-1705] 1776, Griffith, E. (trans.), *The Memoirs of Ninon de L'Enclos: With Her Letters,* J. Dodley, UK.

De Pizan, C. [1405] 1999, Brown-Grant, R. (trans.), *La Livre de la Cité des Dames (The Book of the City of Ladies),* Penguin, UK.

Dokey, C. 2006, *Golden: A Retelling of 'Rapunzel',* Simon Pulse, USA.

Donoghue, E. 1997, 'The Tale of the Hair' in *Kissing the Witch*, HarperCollins, USA, pp. 83-99.

Doody, M.A. 2007, *Tropic of Venice*, University of Pennsylvania Press, USA.

Dundes, A. 1980, *Interpreting Folklore*, Indiana University Press, USA.

Dundes, A. 1997, *Journal of Folklore Research* Vol. 34, No. 3, Indiana University Press, USA, pp. 195-202.

Ellis, J.M. 1983, *One Fairy Story Too Many: The Brothers Grimm and Their Tales*, The University of Chicago Press, USA.

Fee, C.R. 2011, *Mythology in the Middle Ages: Heroic Tales of Monsters, Magic and Might*, Praeger, USA.

Ferdowsi, A.Q. [c.977-1010] 2011, Levy, R. (trans.), *The Epic of Kings*, Routledge, USA.

Foley, J.M. 2005, *A Companion to Ancient Epic*, Blackwell Publishing, USA.

Forster, E. (trans.) 1984, *A Woman's Life in the Court of the Sun King: Letters of Liselotte von der Pfalz 1652-1722, Elisabeth Charlotte, Duchesse d'Orléans*, John Hopkins University, USA.

Fraser, A. 2006, *Love and Louis XIV: The Women in the Life of the Sun King*, Anchor Books, UK.

Fraser, J.G. 1963, *The Golden Bough: A Study in Magic and Religion*, Macmillan & Co, UK.

Frey, A.S., McKee, M., King, R.A. & Martin, A. 2005, 'Hair Apparent: Rapunzel Syndrome' in *The American Journal of Psychiatry*, American Psychiatric Association, February 2005, pp. 242-248.

Galiani, F. [1779] 2012, 'On the Neapolitan Dialect' in Bottigheimer, R.B. (ed.), *Fairy Tales Framed: Early Forewords, Afterwords and Critical Words*, SUNY Press, USA, pp. 89-93.

Garry, J. & El-Shamy, H. (eds.), 2005, *Archetypes and Motifs in Folklore and Literature*, M.E. Sharpe Inc, USA.

Geras, A. 1990, *The Tower Room*, Hamish Hamilton, UK.

Getty, L.G 1997, 'Maidens and Their Guardians: Interpreting the "Rapunzel" Tale' in *Mosaic*, Vol. 30, issue 2, 1997, University of Manitoba, Canada, pp. 37- 44.

Gilbert, S. & Gubar, S. [1979] 2000, *The Madwoman in the Attic: The Woman Writer and the 19th Century Literary Imagination*, Yale Nota Bene, USA.

Ginzburg, C. [1966] 2014, Tedeschi, J. & A. (trans), *Night Battles: Witchcraft and Agrarian Cults in the Sixteenth and Seventeenth Century*, Johns Hopkins University, USA.

Gimbutas, M. 1989, *The Language of the Goddess: Hidden Symbols of Western Civilisation*, Harper Row, USA.

Gimbutas, M. 1993, *The Civilization of the Goddess: The World of Old Europe*, Harper Collins, USA.

Goddard, H.C. 2009, *The Meaning of Shakespeare, Volume 2*, University of Chicago Press, USA.

Goffman, K. & Joy, D. 2007, *Counterculture Through the Ages: From Abraham to Acid House*, Random House, USA.

Gould, J. 2005, *Spinning Straw Into Gold: What Fairy Tales Reveal About The Transformations in a Woman's Life*, Random House, USA.

Goffen, R. 1997, *Titian's Women*, Millard Meiss Publications, USA.

Göttner-Abendroth, H. 1995, *The Goddess and her Heros*, Anthony Publishing Company, USA.

Gonzenbach, L. (collector) [1870] 2004, '*Beautiful* Angiola' in *Beautiful Angiola: The Great Treasury of Sicilian Folk and Fairy Tales*, Zipes, J. (ed., trans.) Routledge, USA, pp. 47-51.

Graves, R. 2011, *The White Goddess*, Faber & Faber, UK.

Gray, N.S. 1972, *The Stone Cage*, Dobson Books Ltd, UK.

Green, T. (ed.) 1997, *An Encyclopaedia of Belief, Customs, Tales, Music & Art*, ABC-CLIO, USA.

Grimm, J. & W. [1857] 2001, 'Rapunzel' in Zipes, J. (ed.) *The Great Fairy Tale Tradition*, W.W. Norton & Company, USA, pp. 489-491.

Haase, D. (ed.) 1993, *The Reception of the Grimm's Fairy Tales: Responses, Reactions, Revisions*, Wayne State University Press, USA.

Haase, D. (ed.) 2004, *Fairy Tales & Feminism: New Approaches*, Wayne State University Press, USA.

Haase, D. (ed.) 2008, *The Greenwood Encyclopaedia of Folktales & Fairy Tales*, Greenwood Publishing Group, USA.

Hale, Mrs. 1869, *The Letters of Madame de Sévigné to her Daughters and Friends (1626-1696)*, Roberts Brothers, USA.

Hale, S. & Hale, D. 2008, *Rapunzel's Revenge*, Bloomsbury Publishing, UK.

Hales, M. 2000, *Monastic Gardens,* Stewart, Tabori & Chang, UK.

Harries, E.W. 1997, 'Fairy Tales About Fairy Tales—Notes on Canon Formation' in Canepa, N.L. (ed.), *Out of the Woods: the Origins of the Literary Fairy Tale in Italy and France,* Wayne State University Press, USA, pp. 152-175.

Harries, E.W. 2001, *Twice Upon a Fairytale: Women Writers and the History of the Fairy Tale*, Princeton University Press, USA.

Harrison, L. 1952, *Rapunzel: An Opera in Six Acts*, libretto Morris, W.

Harvey, C. & Press J. 1991, *William Morris: Design and Enterprise in Victorian Britain*, Manchester University Press, UK.

Heiner, H.A. 2010, *Rapunzel and Other Maiden in the Tower Tales*, SurlaLune Press, USA.

Hettinga, D.R. 2001, *The Brothers Grimm: Two Lives, One Legacy*, Clarion Books, USA.

Hewett, D. 1975, *Rapunzel in Suburbia,* PRISM, Australia.

Hibbard, L.A. 1963, *Medieval Romance in England*, Burt Franklin, USA.

Hill, C. (ed.) 2014, *The Critical Merits of Young Adult Literature: Coming of Age*, Routledge, USA.

Hilton, L. 2002, *Athénäis: The Life of Louis XIV's Mistress, the Real Queen of France*, Back Bay Books, USA.

Holmes, S. 2007, *Letters from Rapunzel*, Harper Collins, USA.

Hudson, M. 2010, *Titian: The Last Days*, Bloomsbury Publishing, UK.

Jones, S.S. 2002, *The Fairy Tales: The Magic Mirror of the Imagination*, Routledge, USA.

Kastan, D.S. 2006, *The Oxford Encyclopedia of British Literature*, Oxford University Press, UK.

Knight, S. 2003, *Robin Hood: A Mythic Biography*, Cornell University Press, USA.

Kolbenschlag, M. 1979, *Kiss Sleeping Beauty Good-Bye: Breaking the Spell of Feminine Myths and Models*. Harper Collins, USA.

Koppelman, C. 1996, 'The Politics of Hair' in *Frontiers: A Journal of Women Studies*, Vol. 17, No 2, University of Nebraska Press, pp. 87-88.

La Force, C-R. [1697] 1999 'Parslinette' in Zipes, J. (ed.), *Spells of Enchantment*, Penguin Books, USA, pp. 115-121.

La Force, C-R. [1697] 2001, 'Persinette' in Zipes, J. (ed.), *The Great Fairy Tale Tradition*, W.W. Norton & Company, USA, pp. 479-483.

La Force, C-R. [1697] 2010, Poupard-Gould, S. (trans. for the author), *Les Contes des Contes, par Mademoiselle de X*, Lightning Source UK Ltd.

Lathey, G. 2006, *The Translation of Children's Literature: A Reader*, Multilingual Matters, UK.

Lanzi, F. & Lanzi, G. 2004, *Saints and Their Symbols: Recognizing Saints in Art and in Popular Images*, Order of Saint Benedict, USA.

Larrington, C. (ed.) 1992, *The Feminist Companion to Mythology*, Pandora Press, UK.

Laven, M. 2004, *Virgins of Venice: Broken Vows and Cloistered Lives in the Renaissance Convent*, Penguin Books, USA.

Lee, T. 1983, 'The Golden Rope' in *Red as Blood or Tales From the Sisters Grimmer*, DAW, USA, pp. 66-95.

Le Guin, U. 1979, *Language of the Night: Essays on Fantasy and Science Fiction*, Ultramarine Publishing, USA.

Le Guin, U. 1976, 'Fantasy, like Poetry, Speaks the Language of the Night', *World*, 21 November 1976, n.p.

Lewis, C.S. 1980, *Till We Have Faces: A Myth Retold*, Geoffrey Bles Ltd, UK.

Lewis, W.H. 1953, *The Splendid Century: Life in the France of Louis XIV*, William Morrow & Co, UK.

Lewis, W.H. 1959, *Louis XIV: An Informal Portrait*, Harcourt, Brace & Company, UK.

Lieberman, M.R. 1972, 'One Day My Prince will Come: Female Acculturation Through the Fairy Tale', *College English 34*, December 1972, pp. 283-395.

Littlewood, I. 2001, *A Literary Companion to Venice*, Penguin Books, USA.

Long, B.A. 2005, 'Rapunzel Dreams of Knives' in *Strange Horizons*, Oct. 17.

Lorraine, R. 1993, 'A Gynecentric Aesthetic' in Hein, H. & Korsmeyer, C.C. (eds.), *Aesthetics in Feminist Perspective,* Indiana University Press, USA, pp. 35-48.

Lurie, A. 1990, *Don't Tell the Grown-Ups: Subversive Children's Literature*, Bloomsbury, UK.

Lüthi, M. 1976, *Once Upon A Time: On the Nature of Fairy Tales*, Indiana University Press, USA.

Magnanini, S. 2007, 'Postulated Routes from Naples to Paris: The Printer Antonio Bulifon and Giambattista Basile's Fairy Tales in Seventeenth-Century France' in *Marvels & Tales,* Vol. 21, No 1, Wayne University Press, pp. 78-92.

Mazzoni, C. 2002, *Maternal Impressions: Pregnancy and Childbirth in Literature and Theory,* Cornell University, USA.

McGlathery, J.M. (ed.) 1988, *The Brothers Grimm and Folktale,* The University of Illinois, USA.

McGlathery, J.M. 1991, *Fairy Tale Romance: The Grimms, Basile, and Perrault,* The University of Illinois, USA.

Michaelis-Jena, R. 1970, *The Brothers Grimm*, Routledge & Kegan, UK.

Middlebrook, D.W. 1992, *Anne Sexton: A Biography*, First Vintage Books, USA.

Monaghan, P. 2009, *Encyclopaedia of Goddesses and Heroes*, ABC-Clio, USA.

Morris, W. 1858, 'Rapunzel' in *The Defence of Guenevere and Other Poems,* Ellis & White, UK.

Muljadi, P. n.d., *Disney Theatrical Animated Features: The Complete Guide*, Paul Muljadi, USA.

Murphy, G.R. 2000, *The Owl, the Raven and the Dove: The Religious Meaning of the Grimms' Magic Fairy Tales*, Oxford University Press, UK.

Napoli, D.J. 1996, *Zel*, Puffin Books, USA.

Napoli, D.J. 2001, 'What's Math Got to Do with It?', *Horn Book*, January 2001 p. 61.

Neemann, H. 1999, *Piercing the Magic Veil: Toward a Theory of the Conte*, Gunter Narr Verlag, Germany.

Nelson, J.K. 2005, *Seeing Through Tears: Crying & Attachment*, Routledge, USA.

Nesbit, E. 1901, *Nine Unlikely Tales,* H.R. Millar, UK.

Norwich, J.J. 1981, *Venice: The Greatness and the Fall,* Allen Lane, USA.

Noy, D., Ben-Amos, D. & Frankel, E. 2006, *Folktales of the Jews, Volume 1: Tales from the Sephardic Dispersion,* Jewish Publication Society USA.

Orleans, C.E, duchesse d' [1652-1722] 1900, *Secret Memoirs of the court of Louis XIV and of the Regency*, G. Barrie, USA.

Rapley, E. 1993, *The Dévotes: Women and Church in Seventeenth Century France*, McGill-Queen's University Press, USA.

Rapley, E. 2001, *A Social History of the Cloister: Daily Life in the Teaching Monasteries of the Old Regime*, McGill-Queen's University Press, USA.

Raynard, S. 2012, *The Teller's Tale: Lives of the Classic Fairy Tale Writers*, State University of New York Press, USA.

Roman, L. & R. 2010, *Encyclopedia of Greek and Roman Mythology*, Infobase Publishing, USA.

Rosenthal, M.F. 1992, *The Honest Courtesan: Veronica Franco, Citizen & Writer in Sixteenth Century Venice*, The University of Chicago Press, USA.

Sexton, A. [1971] 1999, *Transformations*, Houghton Mifflin Co, USA.

Schulz, F. [1790] 2001, 'Rapunzel' in Zipes, J. (ed.), *The Great Fairy Tale Tradition*, W.W. Norton & Company, USA, pp. 484-488.

Schwartz, H. 1985, *Elijah's Violin and other Jewish Fairy Tales*, Oxford University Press, UK.

Schwartz, H. 2010, *Leaves From the Garden of Eden*, Oxford University Press, UK.

Sjöö, M. & Mor, B. 1987, *The Great Cosmic Mother: Rediscovering the Religion of the Earth*, Harper Collins, USA.

Skorczewski, D. 2012, *An Accident of Hope: the Therapy Tapes of Anne Sexton*, Routledge, USA.

Slaughter, G. 1927, *Heirs of Old Venice,* Yale University Press, USA.

Snodgrass, M.E. 2006, *Encyclopedia of Feminist Literature,* Infobase Publishing, USA.

Strauss, G. 2003, 'The Prince' in Beaumont J.M. & Carlson, C. (eds.), *The Poets' Grimm: 20th Century Poems from Grimm Fairy Tales,* Story Line, USA, p. 75.

Somerset, A. 2003, *The Affair of the Poisons: Murder, Infanticide and Satanism at the Court of Louis XIV*, St Martin's Press, USA.

Souloumiac, M. 2004, *Mademoiselle de La Force : un auteur méconnu du XVIIe siècle*, La Force, A.R.A.H., France, trans. privately for the author by Poupard-Gould, S. 2011.

Spaar, L. 1997, 'Rapunzel's Exile' in Datlow, E. & Windling, T. (eds.), *The Year's Best Fantasy and Horror: Tenth Annual Collection*, St. Martin's Press, USA, pp. 315-316.

Spaar, L.R. 2003, 'Rapunzel Shorn' in Beaumont J.M. & Carlson, C. (eds.), *The Poets' Grimm: 20th Century Poems from Grimm Fairy Tales,* Story Line, USA, p. 74.

Stone, K. 2004, 'Fire and Water: A Journey Into the Heart of a Story' in Haase, D. (ed.), *Fairy Tales & Feminism: New Approaches,* Wayne State University Press, USA, pp. 113-128.

Tatar, M. 1987, *The Hard Facts of the Grimms' Fairy Tales*, Princeton University Press, USA.

Taylor, E. 1823, *German Popular Stories*, John Camden Hotten, UK.

Taylor, J.E. 1849, *The Fairy Ring: A New Collection of Popular Tales*, AE. Kearney, UK.

Thelander, D.R. 1982, 'Mother Goose and Her Goslings: The France of Louis XIV as Seen through the Fairy Tale' in *The Journal of Modern History*, Vol. 54, No. 3 (Sept 1982) pp. 467-496.

Tolkien, J.R.R. 1997, *The Monsters & the Critics and Other Essays*, Harper Collins Publishers, UK.

Paradiz, V. 2005, *Clever Maids: The Secret History of the Grimm Fairy Tales*, Basic Books, USA.

Peppard, M.B. 1971, *Paths Through the Forest: A Biography of the Brothers Grimm*, Holt, Rinehart & Winston, USA.

van Dijk, M. 2006, 'Being Saint Barbara in England: Shifting Patterns of Holiness in the Later Middle Ages' in Visser, I. & Wilcox, H. (eds.), *Transforming Holiness*, Peeters Publishers, Belgium, pp. 1-20.

Vellenga, C. 1992, 'Rapunzel's Desire: A Reading of Mlle de la Force', *Merveilles et Contes*, 6.1, Wayne University Press, USA, May 1992.

von Franz, M-L. 1976, *The Feminine in Fairytales*, Spring Publications Inc, USA.

von Franz, M-L. 1992, *The Psychological Meaning of Redemption Motifs in Fairy Tales*, Inner City Books, USA.

Watts, D.C. 2007, *Elsevier's Dictionary of Plant Lore*, Academic Press, UK.

Watts, J., Cockcroft, K. & Duncan, I. 2009, *Developmental Psychology*, VCT Press, South Africa.

Warner, M. 1994, *From the Beast to the Blonde: On Fairy Tales & Their Tellers,* The Noonday Press, Farrar, Straus & Giroux, UK.

Warner, M. 2008, 'Letter to the Editors: Rapunzel, Parsley & Pregnancy' in *The New York Review of Books*, July 17, 2008.

Weideger, P. 2004, *Venetian Dreaming: Finding a Foothold in an Enchanted City,* Pocket Books, USA.

Welch, M.M. 1991, 'L'Eros féminin dans les contes de fées de Mlle de la Force' in Hilgar, M.F.(ed.), *Actes de Las Vegas: Papers on Seventeenth Century Literature,* North American Society for Seventeenth Century Literature, USA, pp. 217-223.

Westfahl, G., Slusser, G.E. & Rabkin, E.S. 1996, *Foods of the Gods: Eating and the Eaten in Fantasy and Science Fiction*, University of Georgia Press, USA.

Willard, C. 1984, *Christine de Pizan: Her Life and Works,* Persea Press, USA.

Wilson, K.M. 1984, *Medieval Women Writers*, University of Georgia Press, USA.

Wintle, J. & Fisher, E. (eds.), 1974, *The Pied Pipers: Interviews with the Influential Creators of Children's Literature*, Paddington Press, USA.

Wolf, S.A. 2008, *Interpreting Literature with Children*, Taylor & Francis, UK.

Yashinsky, D. 2010, *Suddenly They Heard Footsteps: Storytelling for the 21st Century*, Random House, USA.

Yolen, J. 2000, *Touch Magic: Fantasy, Faeries and Folklore in the Literature of Childhood*, August House Publishers, USA.

Zipes, J. 1979, *Breaking the Magic Spell: Radical Theories of Folk & Fairy Tales*, Routledge, USA.

Zipes, J. 1994, *Fairy Tale as Myth, Myth as Fairy Tale*, University Press of Kentucky, USA.

Zipes, J. (ed.), 1994, *Spells of Enchantment: The Wondrous Fairy Tales of Western Culture*, Penguin Books, USA.

Zipes, J. 1999, *When Dreams Come True*, Routledge, USA.

Zipes, J. (ed.), 2001, *The Great Fairy Tale Tradition: From Straparola and Basile to the Brothers Grimm*, W.W. Norton & Company, USA.

Zipes, J. (ed.), 2002, *The Brothers Grimm: From Enchanted Forests to the Modern World*, Palgrave Macmillan, USA.

Zipes, J. 2006, *Why Fairy Tales Stick: The Evolution and Relevance of a Genre*, Routledge, USA.

Zipes, J. 2007, 'Foreword: The Rise of the Unknown Giambattista Basile' in *The Tale of Tales, or Entertainment for Little Ones*, Wayne State University Press, pp. xiii-xvi.

Zipes, J. 2012, *Fairy Tale and the Art of Subversion*, Routledge, USA.

Zipes, J. 2012, *The Irresistible Fairy Tale: The Cultural and Social History of A Genre*, Princeton University Press, USA.

Zipes, J. (ed.), 2013, *The Golden Age of Folk & Fairy Tales: From the Brothers Grimm to Andrew Lang*, Hackett Publishing Company, USA.

Websites & Online

Blackmore, S. 2014, 'Waking from the Meme Dream', Author Website, USA, viewed 24 July 2014,<http://www.susanblackmore.co.uk/Chapters/awaken.html>.

Dixson, A.F. & Dixson, B. 2011, 'Venus Figurines of the European Palaeolithic: Symbols of Fertility or Attractiveness?' Publisher Website, Hindawi Publishing Corporation, USA, viewed 19 February 14, <http://dx.doi.org/10.1155/2011/569120>.

Dundes, A. [1984] 2012, 'The symbolic equivalence of allomotifs: towards a method of analyzing folktales', quoted in Urban Archives Blog, viewed 13 February 2014, <http://cityfantasy.wordpress. com/2012/07/10/towards-a-method-of-analyzing-folktales/>.

Hale, S. 2011, 'Just watched Tangled. Feeling slightly violated' , Twitter post, 9 January, viewed 5 August 2014, https://twitter.com/haleshannon/status/ 23916185586241536

Hughes, S.M. n.d., 'The Sexton Tapes', article in *The Pennsylvania Gazette*, December 1991, Author Website, viewed 25 January 2014, <www. dianemiddlebrooke.com/sexton/tpg12-91.html>.

Cotfield, K. & Hirai, M. (eds.), 2013, 'Interview with Jack Zipes', *Interstitial: A Journal of Modern Culture and Events*, Website, viewed 18 September 2013, USA, <http://

interstitialjournal.files.wordpress.com/2013/05/zipes-interview2.pdf>.

Talalay, L.E. 2009, 'Marija Gimbutas, *The Living Goddess*' in *Byrn Mawr Classical Review 1999.10.05*, viewed 17 July 2013, USA, <http://bmcr.brynmawr.edu/1999/1999-10-05.html>.

Windling, T. 2007, 'Rapunzel, Rapunzel, Let Down Your Hair', *The Endicott Studio for Mythic Arts,* Website, viewed on 24 July 2014,<http://www.endicott-studio.com/articleslist/rapunzel-rapunzel-let-down-your-hair-by-terri-windling.html>.

Films

Tangled, 2010, 3D animated motion picture, Walt Disney Animation Studios, California, USA.

Advertising campaigns

'Rapunzel' advertisement for ghd styling products, from RKCR/Y&R Agency, 2010, viewed 24 October 2010, USA. <http://www.ghdhair.com/latest-tv-campaign/rapunzel>

SECTION TWO:

Persinette

The Rebirth of Rapunzel
Persinette

Written by
Charlotte-Rose de Caumont de la Force (1697)
Translation by Jack Zipes

After a long period of courtship, two young lovers were married, and nothing could equal their ardor. They lived content and happy, and to complete their felicity, the young wife became pregnant. They had strongly desired a child, and their wish was now fulfilled.

Within the vicinity of their house there lived a fairy, who was fond of cultivating a beautiful garden that had an abundance of all kinds of fruits, plants, and flowers. At the time of this story, parsley was very rare in that country, and the fairy had it brought from the Indies. Indeed, one could not find any parsley in that country except in her garden.

Now the expectant wife had a great desire to eat some parsley, and since she knew that it would be difficult to satisfy her wants because nobody was allowed in the fairy's garden, she became so sad and wretched that her husband's eyes could barely recognise her. He kept urging her to tell him what had brought about such a huge change not only in her spirits but in her body, and after resisting for some time, his wife finally confessed that she had a great desire to eat some parsley.

Her husband sighed and was troubled by this desire, which would indeed be difficult to satisfy. Nevertheless, since nothing appears difficult if one is in love, he walked along the walls of the garden day and night to try to find a way to climb over. But it was impossible because they were so high.

Finally, one evening, he saw that one of the doors to the garden was open. He crept through quietly, and, happily, he grabbed a fistful of parsley as fast as he could. Then he left as he had entered and carried the loot to his wife, who ate the parsley greedily. Two days later she felt a desire, even greater than before, to eat some more.

To be sure, the parsley must have been extremely delectable.

The poor husband returned to the garden many times afterward, but in vain. Eventually, however, his perseverance was rewarded, for he found the door to the garden open again. He entered and was extremely surprised to find the fairy herself, who snarled at him because he had been so audacious as to set foot in a place where admission was not simply granted to anyone who thought he could enter. The bewildered young man fell to his knees, begged her pardon, and told her that his wife would die if she could not eat a little parsley, for she was pregnant, and her desire was thus understandable and indeed forgivable.

"Well then," said the fairy, "I'll give you as much parsley as you like if you will give me your child when your wife gives birth."

After short deliberation, the husband promised, and he took as much parsley as he liked.

When the time arrived, the fairy went to be near the mother, who gave birth to a daughter, whom the fairy called Persinette.

She wrapped her in sheets of gold and sprinkled her face with some precious water that she had in a crystal vase, which immediately made her the most beautiful creature in the world. After performing these ceremonies to ensure the child's beauty, the fairy took little Persinette to her home and raised her with the utmost care imaginable. Before Persinette reached the age of twelve, she was a marvel to behold, and since the fairy was fully aware of what fate had in store for the child, she decided to shield her from her destiny.

In order to accomplish her goal, she used her magic to build a silver tower in the middle of a forest. This mysterious tower did not have a door by which one could enter it. There were large and beautiful apartments, so bright it seemed as if the sun penetrated them, but they actually received light through the fire of carbuncles that glistened in all the chambers. The fairy had splendidly provided everything necessary for life, and all the rarest things were gathered together in this place. Persinette had only to open the drawers of her dressers, and she would find the most beautiful jewels. Her wardrobe was just as magnificent as that of the queens of Asia, and she always anticipated the latest fashion. Alone in this beautiful residence, she had nothing to desire other than some company. Except for that, all her desires were anticipated and fulfilled.

Needless to say, all the meals were as delicious as one could imagine, and I assure you that even though she did not know anyone except the fairy, she was not bored in her solitude. She read, painted, played musical instruments, and entertained herself with all the things that a girl knows how to do when she has been perfectly educated.

The fairy ordered her to sleep at the top of the tower, where there was but a single window, and after helping Persinette get settled in this charming seclusion, she departed via this window and returned to her own home.

Persinette continued to amuse herself with a hundred different things, and even when she was merely searching around in her caskets, she felt fully occupied. Indeed, how many people would not like to feel as contented as she was!

The view from the window of the tower was the most beautiful in the world, for one could see the ocean at one side and at the other the vast forest, two sights that were rare and fascinating. Since

Persinette had a divine voice, she loved to sing aloud. This was one of the ways she entertained herself, especially during the hours when she awaited the arrival of the fairy, who came to see her often, calling from the bottom of the tower, "Persinette, let your hair down so I can climb up."

One of Persinette's most beautiful attributes was her hair, which was thirty yards long and did not incommode her at all. It was as blonde as gold and braided with ribbons of all colors. And when she heard the fairy's voice, she would undo her hair and let it fall, and the fairy would climb up.

One day Persinette was alone at her window, and she began to sing in her extraordinary way. Just at this very moment, a young prince happened to be hunting in the forest. He had lost the rest of his company in pursuit of a stag. Upon hearing such a pleasurable voice in this wilderness, he approached the tower and saw the young Persinette. Her beauty moved him. Her voice captivated him. He went around that fateful tower twenty times, and when he could not find an entrance, he thought he would die of agony, for he had fallen in love. But since he was daring, he kept looking for a way to scale the tower.

As for Persinette, she had become speechless. She gazed at this comely man for a long time, but all at once she withdrew from the window, for she remembered that she had heard there were men who could kill with their eyes, and this man's looks were very dangerous.

When she disappeared from his sight, the prince became despondent.

He made inquiries in the nearest village, where he was told that a fairy had built that tower and locked up a young girl within. So he prowled around the tower every day, until finally he saw the fairy arrive and heard her say: "Persinette, let your hair down so I can climb up."

Immediately the beautiful girl began to undo her long plaits of hair, and soon after, the prince saw how the fairy mounted by taking hold of the hair. To be sure, he was very surprised by this unusual manner of making a visit.

The next day, he waited impatiently until nightfall. Then, sure that the hour for the fairy to enter the tower had passed, he stood under Persinette's window and disguised his voice admirably to make it sound like the fairy's, and he said, "Persinette, let your hair down so I can climb up."

Poor Persinette, deceived by the sound of this voice, ran to the window and undid her beautiful hair. The prince climbed up, and when he was at the top and looked at her through the window and saw how exquisite she was up close, he thought he would fall back down to the bottom. Nevertheless, he recovered his natural boldness and jumped into the chamber.

Then he bowed down before Persinette and embraced her knees with ardor, to persuade her of his love. But she was afraid. She cried, and the next moment she trembled, and there was nothing that could calm her, for she found her heart full of all the love she could possibly feel for this prince.

Meanwhile he was saying all the most beautiful things in the world to her, and she responded with a confusion that gave the prince hope. Finally, he became bolder and proposed to marry her right then and there, and she consented, though she hardly knew what she was doing. Even so, she was able to complete the ceremony.

Now the prince was happy, and Persinette grew accustomed to loving him. They saw each other every day, and in a short time she became pregnant.

Since she had no idea what her condition signified, she was upset. Although the prince knew, he did not want to explain it to her for fear of frightening her. But the fairy had come to see her, and no sooner did she look at her than she understood the situation.

"Ah, how unfortunate for you!" she said. "You've made a great mistake, and you're going to be punished for it. Fate has had its way, and all the precautions I took were in vain."

After saying this, she asked Persinette in an imperious tone to confess all that had happened. And Persinette complied, her eyes filled with tears. The fairy did not appear to be moved by Persinette's touching story of love, and taking her by her hair, she cut off the precious braids. Then she made Persinette climb down the tower by means of the braids, and she followed her to the bottom. There she covered Persinette in a cloud that carried both of them to the seaside and deposited them at a spot that was isolated but pleasant enough. There were meadows, woods, a brook with fresh water, and a small cabin made of foliage that was perpetually green. Inside there was a bed made of shrubs, and beside it a basket filled with unusual biscuits that were continually replenished. Such was the place to which the fairy had conducted Persinette, and there she left her after reproaching her severely.

These reproaches seemed to Persinette a hundred times more cruel than her own woes.

It was in this place that she gave birth to a little prince and a little princess, and it was in this place that she nursed them and had all the time in the world to cry about her misfortune.

But the fairy did not find this vengeance sufficient. She wanted to punish the prince as well. As soon as she left the wretched Persinette, she returned to the top of the tower and began singing as Persinette had done. The prince, fooled by this voice, asked Persinette to lower her hair so that he could climb up in the accustomed way. The perfidious fairy, who had expressly cut Persinette's hair for this purpose, let it down for him. When the poor prince appeared at the window, he was surprised and more than a little distressed not to find his mistress, and he searched for her with his eyes.

"You reckless fool!" the fairy said to him. "Your crime is immense. Your punishment will be terrible!"

But the prince shrugged off these menacing threats and responded, "Where is Persinette?"

"She is no longer here for you!" the fairy replied.

And invoking her power, she caused the prince to throw himself from the top of the tower. Although his body should have broken into a thousand pieces when it reached the ground, the only agony he suffered was the loss of his sight.

The prince was horrified when he realised that he could no longer see.

He remained for a time at the foot of the tower, groaning and repeating Persinette's name a hundred times. Then he began groping about and tried to proceed as best he could. Slowly he gained confidence and could make his way in the dark world he now inhabited. For a long time he did not encounter anyone who could help and guide him. He nourished himself by eating herbs and roots that he found when he became hungry.

At the end of some years, he found himself one day more troubled by his lost love than usual. He lay under a tree and was consumed by sad reflection, a cruel preoccupation for someone who deserved a better fate. But suddenly he was wakened from his reverie by a beguiling voice. The first sounds pierced his heart, producing sweet feelings as of old.

"O gods!" he cried out. "It is Persinette's voice!"

He was not mistaken. Without knowing it, he had reached her solitary spot. She was seated at the door of her cabin and singing a song about her unfortunate love. Her two children, more beautiful than the day was bright, were playing a little distance from her. They came upon the tree under which the prince was lying. No sooner did they see him than one and then the other ran and hugged him a thousand times.

"It's my father!" they said at one and the same time, and called their mother. In fact, they made such a cry that she came running, for she could not imagine what the matter could be. Until that moment, nothing had ever happened in that solitary place.

Imagine her surprise and joy when she recognised her dear husband! It is impossible to describe it. She uttered a piercing cry above him and quite naturally burst forth into tears. But what a miracle! No sooner had her precious tears fallen on the prince's eyes than he regained his full vision. Now he could see just as clearly as he had seen before, and all this was due to the tenderness of the impassioned Persinette, who now took him into her arms. He responded with endless hugs, more than he had ever given her before.

It was touching indeed to see the handsome prince, the charming princess, and the lovely children express such ecstatic joy and tenderness. The rest of the day continued just as pleasant, and when night came, the little family finally realised it was time to eat. The prince took a biscuit, but it turned to stone. This miracle caused him to groan with terror. The poor children cried, and the distraught mother wanted at least to give them some water, but it changed into crystals. What a night! They believed this terrible time would last forever.

When the sun appeared, they arose and decided to gather herbs. But to their astonishment, the herbs turned to toads and venomous snakes. The most innocent birds became dragons, and vixens flew around them, glaring in a terrifying way.

"I can't go on like this!" the prince cried. "My dear Persinette, I did not want to find you, only to lose you in such a terrible way."

"Let us die together, my dear prince," she responded, embracing him tenderly, "and let us make our enemies envious by the sweetness of our death."

The poor little children were in their arms, all of them so faint that they were on the brink of death. Who would not have been touched by the sight of this poor dying family? They needed a miracle.

Fortunately, the fairy was finally moved, and recalling at this moment all the tenderness she had once felt for the amiable Persinette, she flew to the spot where they were, appearing in a glittering golden chariot covered with gems. She summoned the now fortunate lovers, each of them at one side of her, and after placing their delightful children on magnificent pillows at their feet, she transported them to the palace of the prince's father, the king. There was no end of rejoicing. The handsome prince, whom his parents had long believed lost, was received like a god, and he found himself quite content to be settled after the torments of his stormy life. Nothing in the world could be compared to the happiness in which he lived with his perfect wife.

Oh, tender couples learn to view
How advantageous it is always to be true.
The pains, the work, the most burdensome worry,
All this will eventually turn out quite sweet,
When the ardor is shared in a love complete.
Together there's nothing a couple can't do,
And fortune and fate will be overcome too.

SECTION THREE:
Books Are Dangerous

The Rebirth of Rapunzel

The Birth of Fantasy

The genre of fiction that we know as 'fantasy' was born on 8 March 1939, on a cold, sleeting spring evening at the University of St Andrews on the east coast of Fife, Scotland. A room full of bespectacled students with bored expressions sat in rows, wrapped in their academic robes, as a thin, ascetic-looking middle-aged lecturer from Oxford mounted the podium.

Up until then, the Andrew Lang lectures at St Andrews University had borne such edifying titles as 'Andrew Lang's Word for Homer', 'Andrew Lang as Historian', and 'Lang, Lockhart and Biography'. So a stir of surprise and amusement ran over the crowd when the guest lecturer announced, 'I propose to speak about fairy tales, though I am aware that this is a rash adventure.'

A few students who had already slipped into slumber awoke in surprise. 'What? What's going on?' one mumbled, blinking around.

'He's going to talk about bleeding fairy tales,' his neighbour told him. 'Go back to sleep.'[1]

'Faerie is a perilous land, and in it are pitfalls for the unwary and dungeons for the overbold,' the lecturer continued. 'And overbold I may be accounted, for though I have been a lover of fairy stories since I learned to read, and have at times thought about them, I have not studied them professionally. I have been hardly more than a wandering explorer (or trespasser) in the land, full of wonder but not of information.'

The lecturer paused and looked around the room, which had settled down into silence again. He was a rather ordinary-looking man, with a high forehead and a long nose, but his voice was deep and compelling, and he had a way of investing certain words with drama and power.

'The realm of fairy story is wide and deep and high and filled with many things,' he went on. 'All manner of beasts and birds are found there; shoreless seas and stars uncounted; beauty that is an enchantment, and an ever-present peril; both joy and sorrow as sharp as swords.'

The Oxford don on the podium that day was, of course, John Ronald Reuel Tolkien, known as 'Tollers' to his friends and 'Ronald' to his wife. He was thirty-seven years old, married, with three sons and a daughter, and Professor of Anglo-Saxon at Oxford University. He had published a children's book two years earlier, *The Hobbit*, which had sold out its first print run of 1,500 books in two months and earned him a nomination for the Carnegie

Medal but had been dismissed by his colleagues with 'surprise and a little pity'.[2]

In the spring of 1939, the world was desperately hoping to avoid another cataclysmic war like the one that had torn Europe apart twenty years earlier. Adolf Hitler had been the Chancellor of Germany for six years and had already annexed Austria and Czechoslovakia. He had also already begun the persecution of Jews, culminating in the vicious Kristallnacht of November 1938, when thousands of synagogues were burnt, hundreds died, and 30,000 Jews were rounded up and sent to concentration camps.

Many of the students in the lecture room that day must have wondered why Professor Tolkien was wasting his time and theirs by rambling on about fairy tales when the newspapers were filled with images of marching armies, hunger strikes and bomb explosions. They were not to know that they were present at what would become one of the most famous university lectures ever given.

Tolkien was a philologist, which quite simply means he was a lover of words. He was interested in their history, their meaning and their power. In his lecture on fairy stories, Tolkien said, 'It was in fairy stories that I first divined the potency of words, and the wonder of things, such as stone, and wood, and iron; tree and grass; house and fire; bread and wine.'

He wanted a word that would describe stories that had all the atmosphere and mystery and beauty of fairy tales, without the implication of those stories being childish or sentimental or patronising—what Tolkien called Pigwiggenry.

'I propose…to use Fantasy for this purpose,' he told his bewildered audience. The word combined both the idea of 'fancy', or the imagination, and the fantastic, what Tolkien called 'the freedom from the domination of observed "fact"'.

At that moment, fantasy as we know it was born.

Of course, like any newborn baby, its genealogical chart stretches far back beyond human records. I like to argue that fantasy is the oldest form of narrative art. As long as humans have had language, we have been telling stories of heroes and quests and battles between good and evil. As Joseph Campbell famously showed in *The Hero with a Thousand Faces*, all human cultures have their story cycle—myths and legends and folktales and oral history—populated with the archetypal figures of the Reluctant Hero and the Wise Old Man, the Companions, the Road of Trials, the Trickster, and the Guardian of the Treasure.[3]

Some critics argue that ancient stories filled with magic, monsters and marvels, such as *The Odyssey* and *Beowulf* and the tales of the Arabian Nights and the Knights of the Round Table, cannot be called fantasy because the tellers of the tales, and their audience, believed fervently that gods and genies and dragons and magic swords did indeed exist. Yet these are the ancestors of fantasy, just as the tale tellers and their audiences are our ancestors.[4]

Tolkien's own immediate influences are well known. He loved fairy tales—especially Andrew Lang's *Red Fairy Book*—read Lord Dunsany in his youth, and discovered the work of George MacDonald and William Morris while an undergraduate, using the prize money for the Skeat Prize for English to buy a leather-bound copy of Morris's *The House of the Wolfings*. Tolkien was well versed in Arthurian legends and Shakespeare (a true fantasist, though Tolkien said he 'cordially' disliked him), and he had read T.H. White's novel *Sword in the Stone* soon after its publication in 1938. He knew Eric Rücker Eddison, author of *The Worm Ouroboros*, though he did not like him, and he had been close friends with C.S. Lewis since they had first met in 1926.

Of these writers of the fantastic, William Morris was the first to set his works in an entirely invented world, distinct from 'long, long ago' and 'far, far away'. For many, the creation of such a 'Secondary World'—another term coined by Tolkien in his lecture 'On Fairy Stories'—is one of the defining characteristics of the genre.

Tolkien would not publish *The Lord of the Rings* for another fifteen years, but by that time the term 'fantasy' was being used, if not very widely.

The Magazine of Fantasy and Science Fiction began publication in 1949, the year before the first of C.S Lewis's Narnia books and five years before Volume I of *The Lord of the Rings*.

When *The Fellowship of the Ring* was finally published in August 1954, C.S. Lewis wrote on the back cover, 'It would be almost safe to say that no book like this has ever been written.'

Nowadays, the term 'fantasy' seems rather like the mythical hydra—lop off one head and another two spring to life. There's science fantasy, dark fantasy, adventure fantasy, historical fantasy and romantic fantasy, not to mention new weird, steampunk, magic realism and that useful umbrella term speculative fiction (first used in 1889).

Let me give the last word to George R.R. Martin, whose latest fantasy novel, *A Dance With Dragons*, sold 298,000 copies on the first day of its release. He says:

> The best fantasy is written in the language of dreams. It is alive as dreams are alive, more real than real… Fantasy is silver and scarlet, indigo and azure, obsidian veined with gold and lapis lazuli. Reality is plywood and plastic, done up in mud brown and olive drab. Fantasy tastes of habaneros and honey, cinnamon and cloves, rare red meat and wines as sweet as summer. Reality is beans and tofu, and ashes at the end…
>
> We read fantasy to find the colors again, I think. To taste strong spices and hear the songs the sirens sang. There is something old and true in

fantasy that speaks to something deep within us, to the child who dreamt that one day he would hunt the forests of the night, and feast beneath the hollow hills, and find a love to last forever somewhere south of Oz and north of Shangri-La.

They can keep their heaven. When I die, I'd sooner go to Middle Earth.

ENDNOTES

[1] Of course, I don't know if it truly was cold and sleeting on this day, but we are talking about Scotland in early spring. Similarly, I have no idea if the university students were bored-looking and bespectacled, or if any of them were prone to slumbering in lectures, but then again we are talking about university students.

[2] This is according to Tolkien in a letter to Stanley Unwin, his publisher at Allen and Unwin, on 15 October 1937. In the same letter, Tolkien says, 'If it is true that *The Hobbit* has come to stay and more will be wanted, I will start the process of thought, and try to get some idea of a theme drawn from this material for treatment in a similar style and for a similar audience—possibly including actual hobbits.' This process of thought led him, of course, to *The Lord of the Rings*.

[3] It sounds like a plot outline for *The Hobbit*, doesn't it? Just remember that *The Hero with a Thousand Faces* was published in 1949, 12 years after *The Hobbit*.

[4] And such a statement also assumes that the readers of modern fantasy do not have their own various beliefs in the mysterious power of magic.

First published in
Seizure, 2011

The Rebirth of Rapunzel

The Birth of Science Fiction

Most lovers of science fiction would agree that it is a literary genre dominated by men. At least until the 1970s, most science-fiction books were written by men, published by men and read by men (as well as by a great many spotty-faced teenage boys).

Brian Aldiss went so far as to describe it as 'all-male escapist power fantasy' written by 'philistine-male-chauvinist pigs'.[1] Jules Verne is usually named as the Father of Science Fiction, with H.G. Wells and Hugo Gernsback often sharing the honours with him.[2]

Yet if we agree that science fiction is a 'literary genre that makes imaginative use of scientific knowledge or conjecture'[3], science fiction was born fifty years before Verne published his first novel; more than ten years before he was even a twinkle in his dad's eye.

The first science-fiction novel was conceived in the imagination of a young woman, barely more than a girl, one wild and stormy night in June 1816, on the shores of Lake Geneva in Switzerland.

'How [did] I, then a young girl, come to think of, and to dilate upon, so very hideous an idea?' she was to write later, when her novel, her 'hideous progeny', finally came to be published.

That girl was Mary Wollstonecraft Godwin, and she was only eighteen years old. She had eloped to Europe with her lover, Percy Bysshe Shelley, their illegitimate son, William, and her step-sister, Claire Clairmont, who was having a tempestuous affair with their host, the 'mad-bad-and-dangerous-to-know' poet Lord George Byron.[4] A melancholic physician named John Polidori rounded out the house party at the Villa Diodati, which Byron had hired for the summer.

Yet 1816 was to be called the 'Year Without a Summer'. The weather was cold and rainy, the skies gloomy and dark with ash from the eruption of Mount Tambora the previous year. 'It proved a wet, ungenial summer, and incessant rain often confined us for days to the house,' Mary recorded in her diary.

There was little to do during a rainy summer in 1816: no TV or DVDs or internet surfing, no Monopoly or Trivial Pursuit or Twister. The five young people (Byron was the eldest at twenty-eight) read, wrote poetry and discussed the news of the day. One day, they discussed experiments by Erasmus Darwin (Charles Darwin's grandfather), who had managed to make a severed frog's leg twitch with a charge of electricity.[5]

The house must have been charged with tension, both sexual and psychological. Sixteen-year-old Mary had known Percy only two months before she had eloped with him,[6] and Percy had abandoned his pregnant wife and baby to be with her. Percy is also thought to have had a few flings with Mary's younger stepsister, Claire, who had just discovered she was pregnant to Byron.

Byron wrote: 'That odd-headed girl… introduced herself to me shortly before I left England…[then] I found her with Shelley and her sister at Geneva—I never loved her nor pretended to love her—but a man is a man & if a girl of eighteen comes prancing to you at all hours of the night…'

Byron had himself fled England after the breakdown of his marriage amid rumours of an incestuous affair with his half-sister, Augusta. He was also bisexual, and many biographers wonder whether he was engaged in a homosexual affair with his young and handsome physician, John Polidori, whom he nicknamed 'Polly Dolly'. John, meanwhile, fell in love with Mary and had challenged Percy to a duel.

One wild, tempestuous night, with rain lashing against the windows, the five sat around the fireplace, taking turns to read ghost stories from a French book called *Fantasmagoriana, ou Recueil d'Histoires d'Apparitions de Spectres, Revenans & Fantomes*—translated into English as *Tales of the Dead*. The book had as its epigraph the Latin expression *'Falsis terroribus implet'*, which—roughly translated—means 'he fills (his breast) with imagined terrors'.

The uncanny tales so stimulated Byron's imagination that he challenged the others to see who could write the most spine-chilling tale of horror. They all grabbed quills and ink-pots and set to work. John Polidori's diary describes the atmosphere of the villa:

Began my ghost story after tea. Twelve o'clock, really began to talk ghostly. L.B. repeated some verses of Coleridge's 'Christabel', of the witch's breast; when silence ensued, and Shelley, suddenly shrieking...ran out of the room...threw water in his face, and gave him ether. He was looking at [Mary] and suddenly thought of a woman he had heard of who had eyes instead of nipples, which, taking hold of his mind, horrified him.[7]

Mary, meanwhile, wrote in her diary:

I busied myself to think of a story—a story to rival those which had excited us to this task. One which would speak to the mysterious fears of our nature, and awaken thrilling horror—one to make the reader dread to look round, to curdle the blood, and quicken the beatings of the heart.

She went to bed late, but:

...when I placed my head upon my pillow, I did not sleep, nor could I be said to think...I saw—with shut eyes, but acute mental vision—I saw the

pale student of unhallowed arts kneeling beside the thing he had put together. I saw the hideous phantasm of a man stretched out, and then, on the working of some powerful engine, show signs of life, and stir with an uneasy, half-vital motion.

She woke the next morning with the story clear in her mind and began writing straight away. Mary had assumed she was working on a short story, but the tale of the scientist, Dr Victor Frankenstein, who 'collected bones from charnel-houses and disturbed, with profane fingers, the tremendous secrets of the human frame', began to grow larger, just like the monster he creates.

Mary's diary entries diminish. On 24 July, she says simply, 'Write my story.'[8]

Mary kept working away at her manuscript for another year, through the trauma of Percy's wife Harriet's suicide, the court battle for custody of Percy's two young children (he was declared morally unfit to have them and they were put into the care of a clergyman), her marriage to Percy three months after Harriet's death, and the birth of her third child, Clara.

Mary Shelley completed the book in May 1817. *Frankenstein; or, The Modern Prometheus* was published anonymously on 1 January 1818 by the small publishing house Harding, Mavor & Jones. It had already been rejected by both Percy's and Byron's publishers. Only 500 copies were printed.

Most people assumed that Percy had written it, since he wrote the preface and it had been dedicated to William Godwin, whom Percy was known to admire. *Frankenstein* was not received well critically, being described by one reviewer as 'the foulest toadstool that has yet sprung up from the reeking dunghill of the present times'.

Two months later, Percy and Mary had to flee England because of threats of a debtor's prison. Within a year, two of Mary's three children would die in Italy, and Percy would die there himself in 1822. She was left an impoverished widow with a toddler, named Percy for his father.

The second edition of *Frankenstein* was published on 11 August 1823 following the success of the stage play *Presumption; or, the Fate of Frankenstein* by Richard Brinsley Peake. This time, Mary was credited as the author. She went on to write many other novels, including *Icarus*, *The Seed of Cain*, and *The Last Man*, the first books to feature ideas of robots, cloning, space travel and an apocalyptic future. Mary Shelley said of her writing, 'Life and death appeared to me ideal bounds, which I should first break through, and pour a torrent of light into our dark world.'

The Birth of Science Fiction

ENDNOTES

[1] Brian Wilson Aldiss is a British novelist and vice president of the H.G. Wells Society. His work has been compared to SF luminaries Isaac Asimov, Greg Bear and Arthur C. Clarke. He published *Billion Year Spree: The History of Science Fiction* in 1973 at a time when the only woman to have ever won a Hugo Award was writing under a male pseudonym (Andre Norton, who won in 1964 and 1967). In *Billion Year Spree*, Brian Aldiss put forth the theory that Mary Shelley was the author of the first science-fiction novel.

[2] Hugo Gernsback founded the first SF magazine, *Amazing Stories*, in 1926, and the Hugos—the world's most prestigious science-fiction achievement awards—are named after him.

[3] *Collins English Dictionary*, 2009.

[4] The famous 'mad, bad' phrase comes from his former lover Lady Caroline Lamb, who—once spurned by him—began to stalk him, sneaking into his house dressed as a pageboy. She grew so thin that Byron said he was being 'haunted by a skeleton'.

[5] Erasmus Darwin (1731–1802) was one of the most distinguished scientists of his age and a friend of Mary's father, the political philosopher William Godwin. Darwin's famous prescription for the disease *pallor et tremor a timore* was, 'Opium. Wine. Food. Joy.'

[6] He had declared his love for her while they picnicked on the grave of her mother, the early feminist writer Mary Wollstonecraft.

[7] Perhaps a little too much opium-eating going on at the Villa Diodati?

[8] The first-ever allusion to the writing of *Frankenstein*.

First published in
Seizure, 2011

The Rebirth of Rapunzel

The Glass Slipper: A Classic Rediscovered

If there is any joy in this world greater than discovering a new book to love, it is rediscovering one that you have loved and lost.

I willingly confess to being a bibliomaniac. This is, according to Maurice Dunbar, 'a victim of the obsessive-compulsive neurosis characterized by a congested library and an atrophied bank account.' Our house is inhabited by books, old ones, new ones, those still waiting to be read, ones that have been re-read a hundred times. There are books on every imaginable subject, for I like to be able to put out my hand and find the answer to whatever question is haunting my curiosity. Most of my books, though, are fiction. 'Fiction is king,' as Francis Spufford wrote so cajolingly in 'The Child that Books Built'; (another book I love). 'Fiction is the true stuff, compared to which non-fiction is just a shadow.'

'We hope,' he wrote, '(that fiction) can bring a fully uttered clarity to the living we do, which is, we know, so hard to disentangle and articulate. And when it does, when a fiction does trip a profound recognition...the reward is more than an inert item of knowledge. The book becomes part of the history of our self-understanding. The stories that mean most to us join the process by which we come to be securely our own.'

It is Spufford's argument that the books we read over our lives, but most particularly the books we read as children, that make us who we are. All of us who are ardent readers will be able to name those books which had the most profound effects upon us at different times of our lives. My memory of my childhood is vague and fragmentary at best, yet I can remember every book I ever read and usually where I was when I read it. As I like to own books, this means I will often hunt for years to find a book that I've read and loved and lost. Since many of the books I read as a child are now out of print, this means I love jumble sales, church fetes, and second-hand bookshops. I love all bookshops, but the old ones have a special allure about them, the hope of stumbling across Aladdin's cave in a box of shabby old paperbacks.

Just yesterday I found a book I have been searching for since I was seven years old. That's thirty-two years of looking. The book was 'The Glass Slipper' by Eleanor Farjeon. I borrowed it from my school library and was utterly enchanted by it. I remember I began reading it on my way home from school (I often used to read while walking home from school, and today, whenever I see a child doing the same,

I always smile with a real sense of warmth and comradeship). I became so engrossed in 'The Glass Slipper' that I walked straight past the end of my street, and only came to myself four blocks further on, when my sister's best friend's mum honked me as she drove past, laughing.

I turned myself about and read all the way home. I finished the book on the way down the stairs to the dinner-table that night, and was as replete and satisfied as any glutton after a king's feast. I borrowed the book again several times, and when I left my primary school for high school, it was one of the things I most regretted having to leave.

Perhaps the best way for me to describe the shaping power this book had on my imagination is to confess I named my daughter Eleanor, and that we call her Ella for short, a name for which I've had a soft spot ever since reading this classic retelling of the Cinderella tale. It would be untrue to say that Eleanor Farjeon and her sweet-faced heroine Ella were the *only* influences on my choice of name. Ellen is a family name, and I've always liked Queen Eleanor of Aquitaine, and often thought I would like a tombstone like hers—she lies sculpted in stone on the lid of her tomb in the Abbey of Fontevrault, holding open a book. It would be true to say that Eleanor Farjeon and this book were *strong* influences, however, which goes to show just what a profound recognition it tripped in me at the age of eight.

The Rebirth of Rapunzel

'The Glass Slipper' is one of the books that began my lifelong fascination with fairytale retellings, and with tales of magic and marvel, one which drives my writing today. It is told simply, but with such wit and humour, charm and playfulness, that it is far fresher than any other version of the old tale I've read. Yet it is not a book that can be bought in any good bookstore—it has been out of print as long as I've been alive. Most people have never even heard of Eleanor Farjeon, yet she wrote more than thirty works of fiction, three plays, thirty-three collections of poetry, and numerous biographies and memoirs. There is an award for children's literature named after her in the UK, and she wrote the words to the hymn 'Morning has Broken', which Cat Stevens turned into a mega-hit in the early 1970s.

Born in 1881, the daughter of a novelist and granddaughter of an actor, Eleanor Farjeon was brought up in a household of books, and encouraged to write from an early age. At the age of eighteen, she wrote the lyrics to an operetta penned by her brother Harry which was performed at St George's Hall in London. At nineteen, she sold her first story for three guineas, a fairytale called 'The Cardboard Angel'. She counted D.H. Lawrence, Walter de la Mare and Robert Frost among her friends, and received the Hans Christian Anderson Medal in 1956.

The Glass Slipper

'The Glass Slipper' was first written with her brother Herbert as a play in 1944, and turned into a book in 1955. Eleanor's love of poetry and song comes through in every line—it has the sort of playfulness with language that is rarely seen nowadays.

'When (Ella) was refused (permission to go to the ball), she clung to the last few minutes of the spilt finery, the hasty scramble out of the house, the little squeaks and shrieks on the slippery path: '*It's freezing! It's freezing! Go carefully! Hang on to me! Stop gripping me! You're tripping me! Oops! Ma was nearly down that time! I'm petrified! I'm paralysed! Stop dragging me! Stop nagging me! I'm dithery! It's slithery! OOOPS! Ma was really down that time! We'll be late, we'll be late! Look alive, look alive! The horses are waiting at the end of the drive...*'

Eleanor Farjeon once wrote of herself, 'I can hardly remember a time when it did not seem easier to write in running rhymes than in plodding prose,' and this facility with rhythm and rhyme can be heard on every line.

It is, of course, a strange and poignant experience, reading again as an adult a book one had loved as a child. The scales of innocence are lost from our eyes; we have inherited a world-weariness along with our wisdom. I always loved Enid Blyton when I was seven, but reading her now to my seven-year-old son, I cannot help grinning when one of her bossy boys says, 'I came over all queer.' I find myself subtly editing as I read, even though I strongly disapprove of trying to modernise old stories, much of whose charm comes from the stiltedness and strangeness of the language.

Reading 'The Glass Slipper' again, I was conscious of the distance between myself as a child, discovering the tale for the first time and being utterly enchanted, and me as an adult wishing Ella would be a little less sweet to her nasty step-sisters. Yet now that I have it in my hand again, I cannot wait to read to my own children, and particularly to my own Ella, the story of Cinderella, 'barefoot, tangle-haired and tattered, but with a face as fresh as a flower.'

First published in
Good Reading, January 2006

The Rebirth of Rapunzel
Stories as Salvation

Part of this article is derived from an early version of Chapter 1 of this book.

I was only a child when I faced death for the first time.

Aged just two years and four months old, I was savaged by my father's Doberman Pinscher in the back garden of our home in the Artarmon veterinary hospital. Tossed like a rag doll, my ear was torn from my head and the dog's fangs penetrated straight through the thin bone of my skull and into the brain. My left eye was missed by a fraction of a millimetre.

Somehow my mother managed to wrest me from the dog's jaws. She wrapped me in towels and ran for help, my four-year-old sister Belinda running sobbing beside her. A young man driving down the Pacific Highway stopped and picked her up. At North Shore Hospital, when the nurses unwound the bloody towels from around my head, he fainted.

My mother was told to prepare herself. I was unlikely to live.

Somehow they patched me together again. My ear was sewn back on, albeit a little crooked. More than two hundred stitches covered my head and face. I must have looked like a tiny Frankenstein's monster.

I did not wake up. My temperature climbed higher and higher, and still I lay unwaking, like a cursed princess. No amount of kisses roused me.

Ten days after the accident, I was gripped by relentless fever, uttering constant high cries, red and floppy as a skinned rabbit. Still no one could wake me. The doctors told my mother I had bacterial meningitis. Think of it as another savage dog, a crazed wolf, pinning me down with its heavy paw. No drugs could release me from its jaws. Prepare yourself, she was told. Few children survive meningitis.

I lay in ice like a glass coffin. I was white and red and black. I had gone away from this world, gone somewhere no one could reach me.

Days passed and still my fever climbed. My small body convulsed.

It's worse than meningitis, the doctors said. It's meningoencephalitis. A wild whirling word, full of holes and spikes. Other words came. Seizures. Toxic. Fatal. I heard none of them.

The doctors wanted to drill a hole in my skull to help drain away the infection sinking its claws into my brain. My mother would not let them. Come back, she said to me. Please come back.

The fever broke. Twenty days after the dog attack, I opened one eye (the other was lost inside a bruised mess of swelling and stitches.) I swallowed some milk. I spoke. A week later I was allowed to go home.

It was not the last time that I would outface death.

The dog's fang had destroyed my tear duct. From the age of three years to the age of eleven, I was in and out of hospital with acute infections and dangerously high temperatures. I could hear the fever coming, a rattling roaring locomotion rushing upon me. I could feel it in my skin. Whitecaps of flame and frost. My body undulating, shrinking, stretching. Fingers like rainclouds. Whirling embers in my eyes. Mocking demonic faces.

I knew the hideous.

Flashes of memory are all that remain to me.

Sitting with my head under a towel, breathing in boiling steam.

A young doctor piercing the abscess with a needle. Screaming with pain.

The taste of pus.

Counting backwards from ten as I sink beneath the anaesthetic. Again. And again.

Proudly telling the nurse that I was very good at spelling, that I could spell anything! Her response: *Spell diarrhoea*.

My sister and brother coming to visit me and telling me, in high excitement, that they were on their way to the Sydney Easter Show.

The Rebirth of Rapunzel

Lying in bed listening for the sound of the ding that meant the lift had arrived. It seemed as if the ding was hardly ever for me.

Some people came to visit me but their little girl had to be taken outside as she would not stop screaming at the sight of me (I was not pretty).

Staring for hours out the one small dirty window. All I could see was a green hill crested with an immense old tree and what looked like a castle. I used to imagine galloping up that green hill on the back of a white horse that would fling out its great wings, leap into the air, and take me away.

Sometimes I would be well enough to get out of bed. I would walk around and around the corridors in my nightie, dragging my drip trolley with me. I'd look in all the doorways at the old, sick people with patches over their eyes. It was an old hospital. At one point the floor sloped downwards. I'd hop on my drip trolley and ride it down the slope. It was the most fun I could have—three seconds of wildness and freedom.

Stories. My only source of sunshine, my only solace. I would read all day and as late into the night as the nurses would let me. I dreaded the light being turned off, I dreaded the empty hours of the night. Once my book was taken away from me, all I could do was lie there in pain, trying to imagine myself back in its pages. Stories were escape. Stories were magic.

Many years later I was to write a poem about my childhood:

SCARS

I bear many scars—the ones I show you
the ones I hide.
There are the marks everyone has
small white nicks
celebrating the meeting of elbows
and the asphalt of the playground
this scar
the boys in class teased me
as they always did. I ran away,
the world distorted with tears
the broken paling in the fence that was my gate
drove splinters into my hand
so I stumbled
the long nail, red with rust,
punctured my knee
tore a hole
where now there is this shiny triangle
of scar.

But that is not the
hieroglyphic
I want to show you.
Anyone might have that.

This was my first,
the tooth-mark of ritual.
I might be named Dog-Slayer,
except the dog almost slew me.

The Rebirth of Rapunzel

You are lucky, people say,
the scars do not show.
I have to part my hair to show this
silky, uneven ribbon wrapped around my head.
It is thick and white
It divides my scalp like lines in a diagram
of the cerebral cortex.

If elders once drew upon the stone with
sharpened stick
driving in the rhythms of their story
each repetition, over decades,
scoring deeper into the rock—
so too do I, tracing the jagged line of
my scars
tell again the story
of my childhood
the ripping apart of times
how my head was held in the jaws of the dog,
the slavering beast of myths,
who wrote these runes upon my scalp.

I do not remember Dog,
who taught me the precarious balance
between worlds.

I do remember a fevered world
pulsing
how the relation between objects is altered—
I am small, I am big

my hand floats a huge octopus
trees growing out of my heart
trees a planet away
sounds roaring, voices never real.

In fever,
time is not divided neatly
but quivers apart
dissolves.

This scar
this dog-emblem
has no power to hurt me with memory
only rarely do I shiver
when I see how faces clench
to see it wind through my hair
the tooth-mark of ritual.

(First published in *Quadrant, March 1994*, and then in Kate's collection of poetry *Radiance*, Magellan Books, 2004)

One day, when I was seven, my mother brought me a copy of Grimm's Fairy Tales. The stories inside were full of wonder and peril and beauty and strangeness. Some made me laugh; others made me yearn to travel far, far away to lands of shadowy forests and towers hidden behind thorns; one or two made me shiver and creep into the sheltering tent of my white hospital blanket. All would come to haunt my imagination.

I read that book so many times the spine broke, pages falling out like white feathers. Of all the tales, it was 'Rapunzel' that fascinated me the most. She too was locked away from the world against her will. She too was lonely and afraid. Her tears healed the eyes of the blinded prince, as I so desperately longed to be healed. The uncanny parallels between 'Rapunzel' and my own life seemed to have some kind of potent meaning. I told myself: One day I too shall escape. One day I too shall be healed.

In time, of course, I was.

At the age of eleven, I became the first Australian to have a successful implantation of an artificial tear duct. A small glass tube, called a Jones tube, was inserted beside my eye, draining fluids down the back of my throat. It needs to be cleared out twice a day and often gets blocked, meaning more steam baths and more antibiotics. Although it does need to be replaced, meaning another trip to hospital, this happens only every five to ten years, instead of every few months.

So I too escaped my tower, my tears healed.

My fascination with the 'Rapunzel' fairy tale—and with its key motifs of the tower, the impossibly long hair, and the healing tears—began in that cold white hospital room. In my novels, the themes of imprisonment and escape, wounding and redemption, appear again and again. Towers are a common motif, as is hair as a symbol of life and renewal (also roses and thorns, blindness and healing, and winged people and creatures).

As I grew up, I used to wonder about the story. Why did the witch lock Rapunzel away? Why didn't the prince bring Rapunzel a rope? Did she ever find her true parents again? I was troubled by the lacuna in the story, the gaps and holes and tatters. I began to cobble these holes together in my mind, weaving a new cloth of fancy.

At last I knew I had to write my own retelling of 'Rapunzel'. Not as a children's book, I thought. 'Rapunzel' is a story about sexual desire and obsession and cruelty. It had to be a novel for adults. I also did not want to write it as an otherworldly fantasy. I wanted to capture the charge of terror and despair that young girl must have felt. I wanted to remind readers that women have been locked up for centuries against their wills in this world.

Our world.

So I decided to set *Bitter Greens,* my Rapunzel retelling, in a real place at a real time. This decision meant I could not use magic to explain all the mysteries in the story—the tower without a door or a stair, the golden fathoms of her hair, the tears that heal the prince's eyes...my imagination caught fire.

But where and when would I set my story? I began to look at the historical roots of the tale, to find earlier versions of the story that might help me. I discovered that one of the earliest versions of 'Rapunzel' was written by a 16th century writer employed as a soldier by the Venetian Republic. Venice! I thought. What a wonderful setting for a

Rapunzel tale. All those towers and walled gardens and dark alleyways. I had always wanted to set a novel in Venice, that most fairy-tale-like of cities...

Yet Giambattista Basile's tale had a different ending. His heroine escapes with the prince and throws three magical acorns over her shoulder that transform into savage animals that first impede and then devour the witch. It was the ending with the healing tears that spoke so powerfully to me. I wanted to know who first told that tale. I had to dig deeper.

That was how I stumbled across the fascinating life story of Charlotte-Rose de Caumont de la Force, the woman who wrote the tale as it is best known. She wrote her story, 'Persinette', while locked away in a convent by Louis XIV, the Sun King, after outraging the royal court with her antics, which included dressing up as a dancing bear to gain access to her young lover. I was enchanted by this story. She was my kind of woman! And the more I found out about her, the more I realised what a gift her life was for a novelist. Charlotte-Rose de Caumont de la Force is one of the most fascinating women ever forgotten by history.

Initially I had planned to use her life as a framing device around the main body of the novel, the retelling of the Rapunzel fairy tale. Charlotte-Rose would have none of that, however. She insisted her tale be the primary narrative thread, and her voice would not let me be until I did as I was told.

La Force wrote her fairy tale 'Persinette' while locked up within the high walls of the convent. It was published in a collection of other tales in 1697, the same year as Charles Perrault's 'Tales from Mother Goose' and the Baroness d'Aulnoy's 'Tales of Fairies'. It sold so well (along with a series of scandalous 'secret histories' of famous people) that she was eventually able to buy her way free of the convent and live the life she had always wanted in Paris. The final line of *Bitter Greens* is: *It was by telling stories that I would save myself.*

My quest to discover the first teller of 'Rapunzel' led me to undertake a doctorate on the subject, with my novel *Bitter Greens* written as the creative component, the theoretical being an in-depth examination of the fairy tale. It led me into spending seven years of my life digging deeper and deeper into fascinating fairy tale lore, wandering through wild tangled forests of story. It led me to discovering the hidden history of the Grimm brothers' fairy tales, and so to another novel. *The Wild Girl* tells the story of the forbidden romance between Wilhelm Grimm and Dortchen Wild, the young woman who told him many of the world's most famous tales.

I first read about Wilhelm and Dortchen's romance in *Clever Maids: A Secret History of the Grimm Fairy Tales* by Dr Valerie Paradiz, which examines the oral sources of the famous tales. Dortchen Wild grew up next door to the Grimm family in the old medieval town of Cassel, in the kingdom of Hessen-Cassel. She was best friends with Lotte Grimm, the youngest child of the family, and had an intense childhood crush on her friend's handsome elder brother. She made an extraordinary contribution to the Grimms' fairy tale collection, telling almost one quarter of the 86 tales collected in the first edition. Then—in the final chapter—Dr Paradiz mentioned briefly that Wilhelm and Dortchen eventually married, after a long betrothal.

As soon as I read about Dortchen and Wilhelm, I knew I had to write a novel about them. I was utterly electrified by the heartbreaking beauty and romance of their love affair and by the stories she told. I never knew that so many of my favourite fairy tales had been told to the Grimm brothers by this one young woman.

Dortchen Wild told Wilhelm Grimm 'Hansel and Gretel', 'The Frog King', 'The Elves and the Shoemaker', 'Rumpelstiltskin', 'Fitcher's Bird' (a very gruesome variant of the Bluebeard story), 'Frau Holle', and 'The Wishing Table and the Golden Ass', about a donkey that spits out gold coins from its behind.

On one extraordinary day—10 January 1812—she told Wilhelm three stories back-to-back, while huddling about the stove in her sister's summerhouse so her father would not know.

The tales she told that day were 'The Singing Bone', about a murdered boy whose bones are made into a flute that then sings to accuse his killers; 'The Six Swans', about a girl who must sew six shirts from nettles, without uttering a single sound, if she is to save her brothers from being swans; and 'Sweetheart Roland' about a girl who escapes from a cruel witch but is then forgotten by her beloved.

On 9 October 1812—the day before the fairy tale collection was sent to the printers—Dortchen told Wilhelm another two tales. The first was about a good sister who is given the gift of spitting gold coins, while her evil sister who is cursed to spit out snakes and toads. The second was 'All-Kinds-of-Fur', a dark and haunting tale about a king who falls in love with his own daughter.

Dortchen was eighteen and Wilhelm just twenty-five. Through the telling and writing down of these beautiful, romantic, and terrifying stories, the two fell passionately in love. However, Dortchen's father disapproved of the impoverished young scholar and forbade them from seeing each other. He did not want Dortchen to marry, but singled her out as the one to stay and look after him in his old age.

Parental disapproval and poverty were not the only things keeping them apart. Wilhelm and Dortchen lived through the bloody turmoil of the Napoleonic wars, and the years of hardship and famine that followed. The collection was first published in 1812, the same year as Napoleon's fatal march on Moscow, and it was a critical and financial failure. Dortchen became the poor maiden aunt, looking after her sisters' children, while Wilhelm and his brothers burnt their furniture for firewood so their hands would not be too cramped for writing.

During this time, Wilhelm began to rewrite the tales, making them simpler, more poetic, more powerful. One of the tales he rewrote was Dortchen's tale of 'All-Kinds-of-Fur'. The 1812 version, written down in haste and rushed to the printers, was word-for-word as she had told it, a terrible tale of incestuous desire and cruelty. The heroine escapes from her father-king, only to be captured again, abused, and ultimately married to a king who seemed very like her father; perhaps, it even was.

Wilhelm rewrote it so that much of the cruelty is reduced. Instead of being dressed in a disguise made of the skins of hundreds of flayed animals, the heroine's cloak is made from only small patches of fur. She is not dragged behind a cart, but lifted gently on to it and taken to safety. The second king does not throw his boot at her head anymore and speaks to her kindly. Most importantly, Wilhelm made it very clear that the second king is not her father. Psychologists call the first account (Dortchen's oral version) a tale of incest fulfilled, and the second (Wilhelm's rewritten version) a tale of incest averted.

Hidden in the revised text was a small salute to Dortchen. Wilhelm described the heroine as a 'Wild deer', capitalising the W in a subtle reference to Dortchen's last name.

It is my belief that Wilhelm rewrote this tale as a gift to Dortchen. He knew that it is the stories we tell that shape our lives, just as much as our lives shape the stories we tell.

Eventually Dortchen's father died, Napoleon was defeated, and the fame of the fairy tale collection grew. Thirteen years after they fell in love, Dortchen and Wilhelm were at last able to marry, and they lived together happily for the rest of their lives.

Dortchen Wild is nothing but a footnote in history, yet her life was full of everything I love in a story. Romance, passion, tragedy, struggle, and, finally, triumph. Most importantly, for me, however, was discovering the hidden history of the fairy tales she told, stories which have haunted me all my life.

Fairy tales endure because their messages—hidden within the metaphoric codes of princes and witches and curses and towers—still speak as strongly and clearly to people today as they ever did. We all have the same dragons in our psyche, as Ursula le Guin once said so powerfully. Our terrors and longings walk through the fairy tale landscape, and through our dreams and nightmares. Fairy tales tell us it is possible to face these fears—the ogres of our darkest imaginings—and triumph over them.

Stories can save us, as I know all too well.

For more about the story of Dortchen Wild, see Kate's novel The Wild Girl.

First published in
Griffith Review, August 2013

The Rebirth of Rapunzel

Fuddling Up My Mucking Words Again

Recently, I was teaching a writing class and asked my students how we could show the trait of shyness in a character.

'She could stutter,' one suggested.

'St-st-st-stuttering is a neurological dysfunction,' I answered. 'A failure of the synapses of the brain to properly connect thought and speech. It has nothing to do with shyness. I'm not shy, as I'm sure you've all noticed, but I've fought all my life with my st-st-st-st…'

Once again my stutter defeated me.

It has always seemed a cruel joke to me that the very word 'stutter' is difficult for many stutterers to pronounce. It is onomatopoeic, an imitation of the halting, repetitive sound made by people with this speech dysfunction. Interestingly, it is not only in English that the word mimics the sound. The Egyptian word for stutter is called *nit-nit*; in Fijian *kaka*; in Turkish *kekelmek*; in Hindi *khaha*; and in Hawaiian *uu uus*.

I have struggled all my life with my stuttering. Not to mention all my other speech impediments.

The Rebirth of Rapunzel

I think I have every language disorder known to speech pathologists. The most exquisitely humorous for those that live with me are my spoonerisms, the common term for what linguists call 'metathesis'—the accidental transposition of letters or syllables. I have real trouble with my 'sh' and 'ch' sounds, so that I will say I am going to a 'shicken chop' instead of a 'chicken shop'. I tell my sons to comb their teeth and brush their hair, and to eat their parrots and keys, and when I'm really cross, I say they have very mad banners.

I'm just glad that, so far, I've not said 'hiss and leer' instead of 'listen here', or 'this is the pun fart' instead of 'this is the fun part'. I think my sons are just daying for the wait.

Spoonerisms are named after the Reverend William Archibald Spooner (1844-1930) who was Dean and Warden of New College in Oxford. Spooner was a small, half-blind albino, with a head too large for his body, and a mind too nimble for his tongue. He is most famous for supposedly saying, 'Which of us has not felt in his heart a half-warmed fish?' when he most certainly meant to say 'half-formed wish', and raising a toast to Queen Victoria with the words: 'Three cheers for our queer old dean!'

His blunders while delivering sermons had the most pious parishioner struggling to contain their giggles. It is said he once intoned, 'Our Lord is a shoving leopard', and another time, while officiating at a wedding, he told a shy bridegroom, 'Son, it is now kisstomary to cuss the bride.'

It is not so funny when you are the one constantly tangling your tongue. When I was in primary school, I used to be followed around by a horde of children chanting 'K-K-Katie, K-K-Katie'. I used to dread my turn to read aloud at school, and often, by the time my turn came, I was so blocked all my tortured mouth could deliver was a sound like a frog being strangled.

As an adult, I have often been deep in serious conversation with someone I've highly respected, and seen them roll an eye as my mouth has mangled yet another magnificently conceived, clumsily articulated sentence. In my mind, the words are mellifluous as honey. In my mouth, they are shards of glass.

The neurological disorder that causes such speech impediments usually manifests itself before the age of three, and is believed to be genetic. However, disturbances to speech fluency can also be caused by damage to the brain (from head injuries, cerebral strokes or brain tumours), or even more rarely, from psychogenic causes such as emotional trauma. I cannot tell you which of these caused my own stuttering and cluttering. Perhaps it was all three. To explain why, I need to take you back in time, back to when I was only just beginning to walk and talk.

It was a bright spring morning, October 1, 1968, and I was two years and four months old.

The Rebirth of Rapunzel

Imagine me riding my tricycle round and round the small concrete yard of the veterinary hospital in the northern Sydney suburb of Artarmon, where I lived with my parents and sister.

My mother was hanging the washing on the line. A large male Dobermann pinscher was chained up nearby. He had been brought in to the vet hospital to be euthanised, but that was the part my father hated most about being a vet. 'No such thing as a bad dog,' he used to say, 'only a bad master.'

My mother was not sure she agreed, which was why the dog was chained.

Round and round and round I pedalled, the wheel squeaking with each rotation. 'I must oil that wheel,' my mother remembers thinking. 'It's enough to drive you crazy.'

Suddenly the dog lunged forward, snatching me off the top of the dinky-bike and smashing me like a rag doll onto the concrete. My mother screamed and tried to drag me from the Dobermann's jaws. The dog would not let go. She struggled to prise his jaws apart, then dug her fingers in his eyes. At last she managed to wrest me away. Holding me close, she ran for the house. The Dobermann chased after her, snarling, and my mother only just managed to slam the kitchen door in his face.

There was no time to call an ambulance. Bundling me up in towels, my mother ran out onto the Pacific Highway and flagged down a passing motorist, dragging my four-year-old sister, Belinda, with her.

Fuddling Up My Mucking Words Again

A young man drove us to Royal North Shore Hospital. There was blood all over my mother's dress, all over the back seat of his car. He helped carry me into the emergency ward. When the doctors unwound the blood-drenched towels from my head, the young man fainted. The dog's fangs had penetrated straight through my skull and into my brain. My right ear was half torn off, my left eye was a swollen mess, and the dura mater of the brain was exposed.

I was in surgery for hours. More than 200 stitches were needed to repair the deep gashes all over my head and face. My mother was told to prepare herself for my death.

I survived surgery, but then did not wake up. My temperature soared. I was packed in ice, a fan blowing cool air on me. Nothing helped. Laboratory tests showed I had meningitis (an infection of the membranes that surround the brain). I was treated with antibiotics, but my temperature continued to rise. For days I tossed in fever, screaming in pain. Eleven days after the dog attack, my mother was told that I had developed encephalitis (an acute, life-threatening inflammation of the brain). I needed surgery to drain the infection away, a procedure that in 1968 was nearly always fatal.

My mother refused to sign the permission slip. She felt that I would be sure to die if they drilled a hole into my brain. The doctors tried to persuade her, but she was adamant. So they went in search of someone to persuade her, leaving her alone with me. My mother sat, holding my small, limp hand. To her astonishment and joy, I opened my one good eye and told her, 'I hungry.'

That was the turning point. Gradually, my temperature dropped. Twenty days after the dog attack, the nurses' report reads: 'Up in playpen. Drinking well from a bottle.' I was allowed to go home at the end of the month.

That was only the beginning, however. Fifteen months later, I was readmitted to hospital. My medical records read: 'Blocked tear duct following savaging by dog Oct 1968. Now discharge all time and recently had infection. Pus expressed from L sac.' It was discovered that the dog's fang had destroyed my left tear duct.

I was treated, but had to return to hospital on February 24, then again on March 17 and March 24. So began a pattern that would re-occur again and again during my childhood. I had developed chronic dacryocystitis (a recurring infection of the tear-duct). My eye wept all the time. The tear duct would become blocked, an abscess would form, my temperature would soar, and I'd be rushed to hospital.

I can still remember the strange, dreamlike sensation that would come over me as my temperature climbed. I'd hear a roaring in my ears, like an ocean inside a shell. My feet and hands would seem huge and clumsy, as if a giant's limbs had been grafted on to mine, and then they would seem very small and faraway, as if I had eaten Alice's cake in Wonderland. Nightmares haunted my sleep.

I had operation after operation at the Sydney Eye Hospital to try to insert an artificial tear duct. They all failed. I was the only child in a ward of little white beds. Given the bed next to the window, I looked out on to a high green hill with a huge old tree rising from its crest, beside a grand sandstone building.

I now know this was a Moreton Bay fig tree growing close to the wall of the Art Gallery of NSW. At the time, it seemed like a magic faraway tree growing beside a castle. I used to imagine galloping up that green hill on a winged horse that would then leap into the air and take me away.

Occasionally, I would be well enough to be let out of bed, and then I would walk around the quadrant in my nightie, dragging my drip trolley with me. I'd look in all the doorways at sick elderly people with patches over their eyes. The hospital was in an old building. At one spot the floor sloped downwards, and I'd hop on my drip trolley and ride it down the slope like a scooter. It was the most fun I had—three seconds of wildness and freedom.

Books were my only source of sunshine, my only solace. I would read my favourite books to rags, and then lie there in my hard, narrow bed, imagining myself into the stories. I began to write my own stories, always filled with magic, adventure and escape from adversity.

Before the accident, I had been a happy child who babbled away. After the accident, I refused to speak. I'd sit on the ground and cry, pointing at the fridge.

'She wants some milk,' my sister would say.

'Use your words, Kate,' my mother would say.

French psychoanalyst Jacques Lacan believed that 'the human condition only truly starts from the moment we enter language'. What does that mean to a child for whom language has become an impenetrable, thorny barrier?

Some sixty million people in the world stutter. Many more have minor disfluency that causes them to hesitate, to stumble and mumble, to umm and aah. Every word we speak calls on 37 muscles and thousands of nerves. It's not surprising that sometimes these nerves and muscles fail us.

Minor disfluencies are part of the communicative process. But for some people, the struggle to articulate words is so profound it shapes their whole life. You could argue that I am a writer because I find the brain-hand nexus so exhilaratingly fluid, compared to my brain-mouth connection which splutters and clutters.

Stuttering is a disruption in the fluency of verbal expression distinguished by involuntary repetitions or prolongations of sounds or syllables. 'Blocking' is the worst of these. This is when you are caught in such an acute muscular spasm that no sound at all comes out. A complete stoppage of speech. I cannot tell you how awful this is.

Fuddling Up My Mucking Words Again

Sometimes you manage a repeated sound: 'St-st-st-stutter.' I am now so adept at these prolonged repetitions that I will say 'w-w-w....marriage', when I want to say 'wedding'.

I had years of speech therapy, including a stay at a stutterer's camp where we were given coupons for food, one of which was taken away every time we stuttered. I would have starved if they had not taken pity on me.

It has been a lifelong battle. Often, people who meet me now do not realise I am always on guard against the tripwire, the tongue-tangler. I have spent my life learning how not to stutter, how not to clutter, how not to metathesise. I try to speak more slowly, to breathe more deeply, to allow time for my vocal cords to catch up with my brain.

Unsurprisingly to me, lots of writers are sufferers. Lewis Carroll (whose utter fascination with wordplay and slips of the tongue is a dead giveaway). W. Somerset Maugham. Margaret Drabble (who I bet is good at Scrabble). Nevil Shute.

Most people take for granted the ability to speak, to argue, to persuade, to command. Yet, for someone like me, words are like lightning balls—dangerous, treacherous and sly. Every day I grapple with words and try to harness their dreadful, electric power to my purposes, to make them say what I want them to say. There is nothing I passionately admire more than a conqueror of words, and nothing that shames me and humiliates me more than my occasional defeat.

For once I begin to stutter and spoon, there is nothing I can do but bow my head, and say, apologetically, 'I'm s-s-sorry, but I'm having a little wouble with my turds today.'

First published in
The Sydney Morning Herald,
November 17, 2012

The Rebirth of Rapunzel

Books Are Dangerous

Books are dangerous.

I have known this ever since I set my bed on fire when I was about four years old. My sister and I had been tucked up in bed, but I wanted to keep on reading. I waited until my mother had gone, and then I created a tent under my bedspread and dragged my bedside lamp inside, the light burning down on the page. Gradually my eyelids sank lower. Gradually my breathing deepened. I fell asleep (it must have been a really boring book to put me to sleep so fast). The paper began to smoulder. Smoke wreathed up. The book burst into flame. So did my bedspread.

My mother has no sense of smell. Luckily for me, she saw the smoke seeping out from under the door and so was in time to save my life.

When I tell this anecdote to school students, I always ask them; 'What do you think is the moral of this story?'

Some good, obedient child will always say: 'Don't read under the bedspread when you're meant to be asleep?'

'No!' I cry. 'I would never say "Don't read". The moral of the story is: Never Read A Boring Book. Read something that'll keep you up all night! Read one of my books (but make sure you use a torch, not a lamp).'

And being obedient children, they do.

I don't remember learning to read. It seemed to happen very easily and naturally. I do remember my first day at school. When my teacher realised I could read fluently, I got to spend the day sitting in a beanbag in a corner of the room, reading my way through the classroom library, while the other students were taught their ABCs. I went home in an absolute fever of delight and told my mother, 'I *love* school.' She was called in to speak to the principal and castigated for teaching me to read. My mother asked: 'How was I meant to stop her?'

The first novel I ever read by myself was *The Lion, the Witch and the Wardrobe* by C.S. Lewis. My sister Belinda and I were staying with our aunt, and she was reading it to us every night. Both Belinda and I were utterly enchanted by the story, and played Narnia all day long. My sister aggravated me beyond endurance by reading on in the story, saying, 'You'll never believe what happens next!' I had to find out. As soon as she put the book down, I picked it up and began to puzzle my way through. Slowly the black hedge of thorns on the page parted, revealing a snowy landscape of dark trees through which the light of a lamp-post glowed…

It all begins with our eyes. Only the centre of our retina has enough resolution to recognise small print. It can see only one word or so at a time. Each word is split up into letters, syllables, prefixes, suffixes, phonemes. It must then be put back together before our brain can recognise it as a word.

The neural networks of our brain then get to work. The phonological route located in the temporal lobe converts letters into speech sounds. The lexical route located in the frontal lobe gives meaning to the word. The limbic system deals with the emotional connotation of words, while the angular and supramarginal gyrusserve link together all the different parts of the brain together…and all in less than one-fifth of a second.

Let's say it a little more simply.

When we read the word 'cat', our brain sees those black marks on a white page, and at once sets to work to understand it.

Our auditory processors give us the sound of the word so that we 'hear' it silently: *kuh aaah tuh*.

Our temporal lobes give the word meaning: a small, furry, carnivorous mammal. Our visual processors create a mental image which will be different for each individual and shaped by their own life experiences (I always see a black slinky creature with glowing green eyes and a hooked tail, but others may see a purring grey tabby or a fat orange tom).

Our sensory processes remind us of the touch of a cat's silky fur, while our limbic system will imbue the word with emotional meaning.

For some, delight. For others, disgust.

All of this happens in a flash, our brains lighting up like globes of white fire.

Meanwhile, our brain is sending out all kinds of signals that spark chemical responses in our bodies—the release of adrenaline if we are reading a thriller, oxytocin if we are reading a tear-jerker. Such chemical reactions can alter our brain's fundamental structure…forever.

No wonder books are so dangerous.

In the novel I am now writing, my heroine Ava is a young woman living in Berlin during the Third Reich. On May 10 1933, in Berlin, more than twenty thousand books were burned by the Nazis. Books by authors such as Sigmund Freud, Alfred Einstein, H.G. Wells, Helen Keller, James Joyce, Leo Tolstoy, and the 19th century German Jewish poet Heinrich Heine who wrote: 'Where they burn books, they will also ultimately burn people.'

Ava asks her father why the Nazis are burning books. He tells her: '"Because books are dangerous! Nothing opens up the mind and the heart like books do, and so they have the power to change the whole world. That's why they are burning books, Ava. To stop us thinking, and feeling, and imagining…" He could not go on. Pulling his handkerchief from his breast pocket, my father mopped his eyes and blew his nose. "That is why we must do all we can to resist them,

Ava. They would make us robots without a soul."'

When I read, the real world disappears and only the invented world of the book remains. It is like stepping through a gateway into another time or another world, like slipping inside someone else's skin. Whilst I am there, I can dance with dryads, or struggle with my own shadow upon an uncharted sea, or huddle in hiding from a Black Rider. I know what it is like to be a rabbit shivering in the heather, watching my warren being bulldozed. I know how it feels to be poor, obscure, little and plain, yet to love with all my heart. Whatever tribulations I suffer in the world of the book, whatever triumphs I win, they change me as if they had really happened. Whatever I learn returns with me to the real world.

In books, I have lived immeasurable lives.

When I was a child, I was such a bookworm that I troubled and bewildered my very bookish parents. I would borrow six books at a time from the local library, and have read them all by the following day. I used to walk home from school reading. I would become so absorbed in the book that I would walk past my turnoff, and some considerable time later look up, finding myself blocks away from home. I'd miss my stop on train journeys. I would not hear my name being called in class. I would read so late at night that I could hear the kookaburras' weird cackle as I reluctantly turned the last pages.

Much of my childhood is a blur, because I spent so much of it with my nose in a book. Elsewhere.

I can, however, remember nearly every book I have ever read, and usually I can remember where I was when I read it.

A Little White Horse by Elizabeth Goudge was first devoured when I was about ten, in hospital. The walls were bare and discoloured, the linoleum was cracked, and the food was watery and tasteless. How I longed to be at Moonacre Manor, in a bedroom with a vaulted ceiling, delicate ribbings of stone curving over my head like the branches of a tree, sleeping in a four-poster bed hung with pale blue silk curtains embroidered with silver stars.

How I salivated at the descriptions of supper: 'home-made crusty bread, hot onion soup, delicious rabbit stew, baked apples in a silver dish, honey, butter the colour of marigolds, a big blue jug of warm mulled claret, and hot roasted chestnuts folded in a napkin.' Over the course of the next few chapters, Maria feasts on sausages, coddled eggs (I did not know what coddled eggs were but they sounded so delicious!), veal-and-ham-and-egg pie, cinnamon syllabub, plum cake, saffron cake, meringues, almond fingers, lemon curd sandwiches, gingerbread ...in my imagination I feasted, and so the paucity and insipidity of the food on my hospital tray was forgotten.

A lot of the books that meant the most to me when I was a child were read in hospital. A childhood accident which destroyed my left tear duct meant that I was in and out of the emergency ward constantly. *The Secret Garden* By Frances Hodgson Burnett, *Cue for Treason* by Geoffrey Trease, *The Apple-Stone* by Nicholas Stuart Gray and *The Witch's Brat* by Rosemary Sutcliff were all books my mother brought me from our local public library. I devoured them hungrily while lying in my narrow metal bed, tucked in tight with hospital corners, a patch over one eye. Always I loved stories of adventure and mystery and magic. My body was kept prisoner by railings and intravenous drips and monitors, but my mind could roam free. It does not matter how awful real life is—there is always a way to escape it through the pages of a book.

The summer I read *The Dark is Rising* by Susan Cooper was scorching hot, bare-legs-sticking-to-the-vinyl-car-seat hot. I can still remember the chills that ran all over my body as I read the opening scenes: the sky darkens, the storm gathers, and Will hears the whispered words, 'The Walker is abroad…this night will be bad and tomorrow will be beyond imagining…'

I read *Till We Have Faces: A Myth Untold* by C.S. Lewis in the old frangipani tree in the garden of my great-aunts' old fibro cottage, surrounded by sweet summery smell of the flowers, but inhaling instead the 'temple-smell of blood…and burned fat and singed hair and wine and stale incense…the Ungit smell.'

The very first teenage party I was ever invited to, I spent the evening hidden behind the curtain in a window-seat reading *Precious Bane* by Mary Webb, a book I had discovered on the host's bookshelf. While everyone else drank and smoked and danced and snogged, and the music thump-thump-thumped, I sat with harelipped Prue and listened to 'a still evening with the snow all down, and a green sky, and lambs calling…and the crying of the mere when the ice is on it…' and the sound of drowned bells coming from under the water.

Leo Tolstoy's *Anna Karenina* was read on a train, after my parents' divorce. The book is full of rocking motion, and dark tunnels, and the shrieking of brakes.

I have read in boats and on beaches and in baths, in trees and on trains and in taxis, in planes and on pony-back and in parks, in cars and bars and spas and bazaars (all true!) I read upside-down and back-to-front if I have to (the words, not me).

However, reading alone, late at night, is my favourite way. It is such an acute and secret pleasure. All is quiet and dark. Shadows lean over you, but the small light that you read by is a golden globe of protection, a little sun that shines on a multitude of worlds in which anything might happen.

Books are a true kind of magic, and that is why they are so dangerous and so essential.

First published in
The Simple Act of Reading edited by
Deborah Adelaide, Random House, 2015

The Rebirth of Rapunzel

Rapunzel in the Antipodes

I have spent the last half a dozen years immersed in the study of 'Rapunzel'.

I began only by knowing that something about this fairy tale troubled and fascinated me, and that I wanted to retell the story in a way that would resolve some of the problems in the tale—at least for me.

I first read 'Rapunzel' as a little girl in hospital. My left tear duct had been damaged in an accident when I was a toddler, and—unable to control my tears—I was constantly in hospital with life-threatening infections.

I felt a strong connection to Rapunzel. We were both girls locked away from the world against our will. We were both lonely and afraid. Yet my tears made me desperately ill and half-blind. Rapunzel's tears healed her lover's blindness and made him well. Rapunzel's story gave me hope: one day I too shall escape; one day I too shall be healed.

As I grew up, I used to wonder about the story. Why did the witch lock Rapunzel in a tower? Why did she have to climb Rapunzel's hair? Why didn't the prince just bring Rapunzel a rope? I was troubled by the lacuna in the story, the gaps and holes and tatters. I began to cobble these holes together in my mind, weaving a new cloth of fancy. That cloth of fancy became my novel *Bitter Greens* and my doctoral exegesis, 'The Rescue of Rapunzel'.

When I began working on 'Rapunzel', I thought I was alone in my fascination. I came to realise that there were many other reimaginings of the tale. Oddly, the tale has been very popular among Australian authors. Not including myself, I have found nine—a potent fairy tale number.

The first Australian creative response to the tale was by the poet Dorothy Hewett, who wrote a remarkable collection of poetry in the 1970s called *Rapunzel in Suburbia*. One of the poems, 'Grave Fairytale', is a direct response to the Rapunzel fairy tale. In this poem the witch is described as 'there when I woke, blocking the light / or in the night, humming, trying on my clothes. / I grew accustomed to her; she was as much a part of me / as my own self.'

When the prince climbs Rapunzel's hair 'his foraging hands tore me from neck to heels: the witch jumped up my back and beat me to the wall. / Crouched in a corner I perceived it all, / the thighs jack-knifed apart, the dangling sword thrust home, pinned like a specimen—to scream with joy.' The union of the witch and the prince is described in animalistic terms—they are 'hunch-backed, hairy-arsed', and 'as she ran four-pawed across the light, the female dropped coined blood spots on the floor.'

Rapunzel cuts her own hair so that the prince should fall. 'His mouth, like a round O, gaped at his end...he clawed through space.' Rapunzel is left 'bald as a collaborator...in the thumb-nosed tower. / And the witch...sometimes I idly kick a little heap of rags across the floor. I notice it grows smaller every year.'

Her book came out in 1975, four years after Anne Sexton's highly influential book of fairy tale poems, *Transformations*. Although I feel it highly likely that Hewett was influenced by Sexton, like so many other poets of the times, the two Rapunzel poems are very different. Sexton tells the story of a lesbian love affair between an older and a younger woman, in which the witch is inevitably betrayed and abandoned. However, for Hewett, the witch is a rapacious and voracious force who uses a girl's youth and beauty as bait to seduce the prince herself. The narrative energy of the poem comes from the girl's journey away from helpless and naïve prisoner to a force of feminine power herself.

In 1984, Kerryn Goldsworthy grappled with the tale in a story entitled 'Rapunzel, Rapunzel' and published in *Meanjin*. It was sub-titled 'A Story After Angela Carter', an acknowledgement to the highly influential book of short stories,

'The Bloody Chamber', published in 1975. The story is divided into three parts, told, in turn, from the point of view of the sorceress, the prince and Rapunzel. Rapunzel is described as 'beauty, growth, new life' and the sorceress's magic is 'the delicate compounds of herbs and words my customers would use to gain their heart's desire.' After the sorceress cuts the braid of her hair and casts Rapunzel out into 'a wild, sad place', the girl was 'a spoilt, wrecked, stubbly thing.' At the end, the sorceress lives 'as I had always lived before she was born, beyond good and evil, beyond love.'

In Rapunzel's section, the girl reveals she betrayed herself to the sorceress on purpose. 'You will see this moment is the centre of my story, like the whorl at the heart of the marble, around which everything spins when you flick your thumb... Because I wanted something to happen...I flicked my thumb and sent the marble of my future spinning off out of the circle, away from the game.' In this way, Goldworthy's story seems to link back to the ancient myths embedded in the heart of the story: Rapunzel as a force for growth and change, the sorceress the dark feminine who must be overcome.

In 2005, Juliet Marillier published a short story entitled 'Let Down Your Hair' which begins 'The price of my future was a bunch of lettuce.' The girl is not taken by the witch for 'sheer wickedness... she needed me to do a job.' The witch's task was to watch a pot, 'an iron cauldron hanging from a three-legged stand...as she stirred her bubbling brew, the witch muttered stories.' In this brew, the girl sees 'crowns and swords, goblets and gauntlets, nooses and necklaces ...' The witch tells her that 'stirring this pot is the most important job in the world. Let the fire die down, let the soup cool and congeal, and something irreplaceable is lost.'

In this way, the witch's pot is linked to what Tolkien called 'The Cauldron of Story', which 'has always been boiling, and to it have continually been added new bits, dainty and undainty.'

A woodcutter passes by, but is seduced away by the witch, and the girl is left alone to stir the pot. Time passes and the girl grows older. There are grey hairs among the gold. At last the woodcutter comes back, his face lined and weary, his young strength grown crooked. They cannot be together, for he is not strong enough to scale the wall. It is only when the cauldron shows the imprisoned woman a key and she plunges her hand in to the hot liquid to seize it that she can at last unlock the door. She does not leave the tower, though, for her task of stirring the pot is too important. She and the woodcutter simply leave the door unlocked. Marillier's story celebrates the coming of age and wisdom, and the importance of storytellers keeping old tales alive.

In 2009, three very different retellings were published.

The Rebirth of Rapunzel

One, by the Australian visual artist Deborah Klein, is a short fragment of a tale only a page long, and accompanied by one of the artist's mysterious and beautiful paintings. It tells the story as if in a traditional tale for children, beginning 'There was once a girl who had lived all of her life in a tall tower in the middle of a dark and almost impenetrable wood.'

The girl of Klein's story was, however, locked up by her father for a reason no-one can 'exactly remember'. In this way, Klein's story links back to earlier traditions of the Maiden in the Tower tale in which the tower acts as a symbol for patriarchal dominance and subordination. 'A handsome prince…on a milk white steed' rides by to look, and the girl entices him up by throwing out her hair for him to climb. The prince boasts about all his deeds of derring-do, including 'countless maidens he had wooed and won'. But none could compare to her because 'none…had such long and wondrous hair'. The girl wants to ride out and have adventures with him, but since this would mean she had to cut off her hair he begs her not to do so.

When he wakes in the morning, the girl has cut her braid and is riding off on his milk white steed. She jerks the braid so he cannot climb down after her. 'How on earth am I to escape?' he cries / 'Grow your own hair', she answers as she 'rode off into the sunset'.

Also published in 2009 was Margo Lanagan's tale 'The Golden Shroud', which is told from the point of view of the prince. The maiden's hair is the most striking image in this story—described as golden light, 'motionless fire, a weighty plaited sun', 'rippling cloth-of-gold', 'material for a thousand gorgeous bird-nests', 'a sunlit spillage', and, most tellingly, 'a cruelty to her'.

When the prince is imprisoned by the witch, white-faced above her black dress, 'her hand like a knot of bones', a lock of the maiden's hair rescues him, 'a loose spiral of moving gold. The end of it sat up like a serpent's head above its coil.' With the lock of hair's help, the prince rescues the maiden and then defeats the witch: 'a storm of golden hair...bound the horror in a golden shroud.' Hair has always been a symbol of life and strength and regeneration. In this tale, it becomes too an instrument of death and revenge.

The last story to be published in 2009 was Garth Nix's humorous children's story, 'An Unwelcome Guest', which frames Rapunzel as an unpleasant teenage girl and the witch as a long-suffering hostess trying to trick her into leaving so she can get back to making frog jelly. It isn't until the witch cuts the braid and releases her from the spell of a Bad Old One that Rapunzel can go back to being a normal kid. Describing his inspiration for the tale, Nix has said that he has 'always had an interest in dark woods, fleeting shadows, and misunderstood eccentrics whom the world had labelled "evil" without attempting to understand their motives.'

Angela Slatter is another Australian writer whose work is enriched by myth and fairy tale. Her story 'Little Radish' was published in 2010, and her heroine longs for the solitude and silence of a tower: 'I imagined an incomparable stillness, held in by granite, a barrier that nothing could penetrate.' In her search to find that solitude, Rapunzel meets an old woman named Sybille who gives her the key to an invisible tower and the spell to bring it into sight. The girl protests that she is not a witch. 'You're a woman, aren't you?' is the answer. The girl lives peacefully for a while, until the arrival of the prince. They seduce each other, but in time the prince says that he must go. In her anger, Rapunzel pushes him from the tower and he is blinded. She then gives birth to a son, with Sybille's help, but the child is stillborn. The wise woman puts the dead baby in a crystal casket and tells Rapunzel to go in search of her prince. 'People, said Sybille, are not meant to be alone...solitude was for those broken beyond repair.'

In the end Rapunzel finds her prince and finds him much changed. 'I did not truly see until my sight was gone, nor had I listened to my heart nor the hearts of others until my own had been wounded,' the prince says. As Rapunzel gives him their dead son the child moves and cries. 'So live the blind king, his wounded wife, and their twice-born son,' the story ends.

James Bradley published a novella entitled 'Beauty's Sister' in 2013. The story is told from the point of view of Rapunzel's younger sister Juniper, dark and wild and free in contrast to the imprisoned golden beauty. As Juniper grows, she becomes obsessed with both her sister in the tower and the witch who put her there: 'There was something black inside her, something cold and cunning, and…power pleased it, made it stronger.' In the end, Juniper betrays her sister and her lover, who had once been Juniper's, and in doing so loses them both.

Finally, Danielle Wood has included a retelling of 'Rapunzel' entitled 'Lettuce' in her 2014 short story collection, *Mothers Grimm*. The story is set emphatically in contemporary Australia, with the opening line describing 'a species of Arnott's biscuit called the Orange Slice'. The action takes place amongst a group of women who are all taking a course in pre-natal yoga together. They've known each other for years, and so their curiosity is aroused when a new woman joins the group. Her beauty, her confidence, and the sense of mystery about her causes 'a disturbance, just a small one, somewhere deep in (Meg's) private universe.' Later, Meg sees the mystery woman steal a mouthful of lettuce from the display garden at the nursery Meg owns with her husband. Meg has laboured over the garden: 'the icebergs were building their own hearts, inner leaves folding like pale green hands around a secret.' The theft of the lettuce leaf makes Meg feel 'unaccountably violated'; later, when the mysterious unnamed woman abandons her newborn baby in the hospital, Meg suggests the nurses call the child 'Lettuce'. The woman's abandonment of her child sets up an uncomfortable dissonance for Meg, who struggles with her own loss of identity as a mother and wife.

It is interesting to conjecture why Rapunzel has proved so inspiring to Australian authors. One could posit a theory that this tale of imprisonment and escape has some resonance in a post-colonial imaginative landscape, in a country whose early role in Western culture was as a prison. One could say that Rapunzel's struggle to break free of a suffocating mother figure is, perhaps, a metaphor for Mother England.

I would not argue so, however. For me, the mystery and the power of fairy tales is that they are shapeshifters, constantly changing and being transformed while still carrying within them the symbols and structures of far older stories. Although it is true that fairy tales speak in metaphoric codes, each teller reads those codes a little differently and, in retelling the tale, gives it deeper and wider meanings, allowing the story new relevance to each new audience.

In the final pages of 'Beauty's Sister', James Bradley's heroine Juniper says: 'I have heard many versions of what happened next…Perhaps they are all true. This is what stories do, after all: go out into the world, become real. We think we tell them, but more they tell us, make us theirs.'

First presented as a paper at
Australian Genre Crossings Symposium
11 October 2013
State Library of Queensland
https://genrecrossings2013.wordpress.com/program/

The Rebirth of Rapunzel

In the Tower

Walled in my old stone tower
the bitter taste of tears
always in my throat
only a slit to put my eye to
yet how full of change is that sky
I watch the stars wheel past
seasons turning and turning
the one tree on that faraway hill
once more bursts into life
green in the shadows
golden in the light

Walled in my silent tower
how can I frame the words
to tell my story
my heart is a riddle
green sickness in my soul
loneliness the heaviest burden
how I long to slip free
of this empty shadowed tower
fly on muffled wings like the owl
white against the thorns
black against the moon

The Rebirth of Rapunzel

Walled in my cold stone tower
I conjure a steed from flame
An invisible cloak from ashes
A frail ladder from cobwebs
I make a dagger from ice
A key from bone and wishes
I spin a song from the silence
One day someone shall sing my refrain
Green in the shadows
Golden in the light

Free of my shadowy tower
We shall bind ourselves together
With tendrils of green
With tresses of gold
We shall build a castle of light and air
And banish silence with song
Together we'll dance in the forest
White against the thorns
Black against the moon

About Kate Forsyth

Kate Forsyth wrote her first novel at the age of seven, and is now the internationally bestselling and award-winning author of thirty-six books, ranging from picture books to poetry to novels for both adults and children. She was recently voted one of Australia's Favourite 15 Novelists, and has been called 'one of the finest writers of this generation'. She is also an accredited master storyteller with the Australian Guild of Storytellers, and has told stories to both children and adults all over the world.

Her most recent books for adults include historical novels *The Beast's Garden* (2015) and *The Wild Girl* (2013).

The Beast's Garden is a retelling of the Grimm's 'Beauty and The Beast' set in Nazi Germany. The book is a compelling and beautiful love story, filled with drama, intrigue and heartbreak, taking place between Kristallnacht in late 1938 and the fall of Berlin in 1945.

The Wild Girl tells the true, untold love story of Wilhelm Grimm and Dortchen Wild, the young woman who told him many of the world's most famous fairy tales. Set during the Napoleonic Wars, *The Wild Girl* is a story of love, war, heartbreak, and the redemptive power of storytelling, and was named the Most Memorable Love Story of 2013.

Kate is probably most famous for *Bitter Greens* (2012), a retelling of the Rapunzel fairy tale interwoven with the dramatic life story of the woman who first told the tale, the 17th century French writer, Charlotte-Rose de la Force. *Bitter Greens* has been called 'the best fairy tale retelling since Angela Carter', and won the American Library Association Award for Best Historical Novel of 2015. It was also nominated for a Norma K. Hemming Award, the Aurealis Award for Best Fantasy Novel, and a Ditmar Award. Having already sold more than a quarter of a million copies world-wide, it was subsequently released in the US in September 2014.

Since *The Witches of Eileanan* was named a Best First Novel of 1998 by Locus Magazine, Kate has won or been nominated for numerous awards, including a CYBIL Award in the US. She's also the only author to win five Aurealis awards in a single year, for her **Chain of Charms** series—beginning with *The Gypsy Crown*—which tells of the adventures of two Romany children in the time of the English Civil War. Book 5 of the series, *The Lightning Bolt*, was also a CBCA Notable Book. Her most recent books for children include the bestselling fantasy adventure series **The Impossible Quest.**

Kate's books have sold more than a million copies internationally, having been published in 17 countries including the UK, the US, Russia, Germany, France, Japan, Turkey, Spain, Italy, Poland and Slovenia. She has a doctorate in fairy tale studies from at the University of Technology, having already completed a BA in Literature and a MA in Creative Writing.

Kate is a direct descendant of Charlotte Waring, the author of the first book for children ever published in Australia, *A Mother's Offering to her Children*. She lives by the sea in Sydney, Australia, with her husband, three children, and many thousands of books.

Kate is also a proud ambassador for the two following wonderful initiatives to help disadvantaged children change their worlds through the power of books and reading—Room to Read and The Pyjama Foundation.

Look for our ebook-only collection and more FableCroft books at our website:

http://fablecroft.com.au/

Havenstar by Glenda Larke
Pratchett's Women by Tansy Rayner Roberts
50 Roman Mistresses by Tansy Rayner Roberts
The Bone Chime Song and Other Stories by Joanne Anderton
Guardian by Jo Anderton
The Mocklore Chronicles by Tansy Rayner Roberts
Splashdance Silver
Liquid Gold
Ink Black Magic
Isles of Glory trilogy by Glenda Larke
The Aware
Gilfeather
The Tainted
Worlds Next Door edited by Tehani Wessely
Australis Imaginarium edited by Tehani Wessely
After the Rain edited by Tehani Wessely
Epilogue edited by Tehani Wessely
One Small Step edited by Tehani Wessely
Phantazein edited by Tehani Wessely
Cranky Ladies of History
edited by Tansy Rayner Roberts & Tehani Wessely
Insert Title Here edited by Tehani Wessely
Focus 2014: highlights of Australian short fiction edited by Tehani Wessely
Focus 2013: highlights of Australian short fiction edited by Tehani Wessely
Focus 2012: highlights of Australian short fiction edited by Tehani Wessely
Canterbury 2100: Pilgrimages in a New World edited by Dirk Flinthart
Striking Fire by Dirk Flinthart
Path of Night by Dirk Flinthart
"Sanction" by Dirk Flinthart
"Flower and Weed" by Margo Lanagan
To Spin a Darker Stair
by Catherynne M Valente & Faith Mudge
Coming Soon:
In Your Face edited by Tehani Wessely
Bounty and the Void by Tansy Rayner Roberts

www.ingramcontent.com/pod-product-compliance
Lightning Source LLC
Chambersburg PA
CBHW021620030826
48979CB00034B/492

9780992553494